THE SWALLOWED WORLD

BOOK ONE

TYLER BUMPUS

OMEGA POINT Books

THE SWALLOWED WORLD: BOOK ONE —

THE ETERNAL SEASON

An Omega Point Books Trade Paperback Book

Copyright © 2016 by Tyler Bumpus

Cover art by Amir Zand © 2018 Amir Zand

Chapter illustrations by Kyle Bumpus © 2018 Kyle Bumpus

ISBN-13: 978-0-6929-0726-9

ISBN-10: 06-929-0726-2

The ETERNAL SEASON

CONTENTS

APPENDICES

BOOK TWO PREVIEW

For Larry Delbert Bumpus

Lord of Movie Goof-Hunting.
Wielder of Mighty BBQ Tongs.
Who, against his sweet nature
(but to my glee) has a soft spot—
Clint, Hackman, Jack, et al—
for scoundrels and monsters.

The blood-dimmed tide is loosed, and everywhere
    The ceremony of innocence is drowned;
    The best lack all conviction, while the worst
    Are full of passionate intensity.

— W. B. YEATS

ARTIFACT B-013983
"FL TERRITORY ATLAS"

Cat. Replica (painted peatsheet)

Found Sacramento ruins Y43, DE

Bloc Archive 013983

KEY (CONJECTURAL)

★ — TERRITORIAL CAPITAL

○ — MAIN CITY/SETTLEMENT

● — MINOR PROVINCE (?)

⟜ — TRANS-PENINSULA CANAL

▬ — CANAL BRINKGATE

━ — "THE BRINK"
    (BLOC PROTECTORATE BORDERLINE)

🦎 — GATORBRID BREEDING ZONES (?)

MAP

Researcher's Note on Artifact B-013983:

It is widely known that most enigmatic first editions of
the so-called *Swallowed World* tome are lost (any surviving
the Virgin Army's bonfires now well out of circulation).
Though only a hand-made replica of one such relic, this
crude map of late Florida Territory likewise predates the
Great American Rift—in fact, our entire Diluvian Era—
by decades. Making Artifact B-013983, like its missing
genuine counterpart, a riddle of historical and (arguably)
oracular significance.

YEAR 55, DE
(Diluvian Era)

PART 1

PRESSURES

THE BORDER GUARDSMEN ransacking Albert's ship reminded him of beetles—not sweet, extinct ladybugs, but those big ugly bastards that lived off shit. Mud-caked boots scurried across his deck with mindless energy; helmets and armor of deactivated chamelo plating refracting light like scarab shells.

One zealous bordie tore open a storage hatch on the cabin bulkhead, avalanching life jackets, flares and sea dye markers to the deck.

"Break it you buy it, shithead." Albert Fountain lounged on a ferry bench, cutting an arresting figure for a man pushing forty: lean and tall in cargoes and unbuttoned panama shirt, scathing hawklike eyes, dapper dark hair just dusted with regal gray. "Save yerself the trouble and scan the damn ship, huh?"

"Scatter-rayin' the hull *would* be easier..." Leering through his helmet's holographic HUD visor, the borderman crunched a fallen dye tube beneath his boot; a biolume stain blooming on the wood. "But ain't half as fun."

"That's cute." Albert turned to the patrol skiff floating off the starboard side, cupping hand to mouth: "Yo, Fredy! Yer kiddies are finger-painting!"

The squad leader squinted back at him through harsh Floridian sunlight. The shortest borderman on the skiff, arms crossed and legs splayed to affect an aura of command. His own mishmash attire—rank insignias flaunted like scout badges; silly non-regulation epaulettes and military cords; a one-shoulder cape woven in neo-Latino designs—all draped over his chamelo body armor. The photochemical camo was needlessly activated, mimicking algae-blotched concrete of the Canal wall behind him.

"*Well?*" Albert demanded, rocking forward to his feet.

Like some pompous, high-tech conquistador, Fredy only shrugged back.

A scrawny black man stormed from the cabin now in a huff, aloha shirt clinging to his sweaty cocoa chest. He halted a meter from Albert on deck to survey the hoopla, rubbing silvery stubble, finally inquiring: "Allie, whatta *hell* happenin'?"

"We're cool, Remy," Albert assured his charter captain (and accomplice). "Just infested with assholes."

Dark features scrunched in displeasure. "They movin'

below deck," the older man whispered. Bad news punctuated by a fresh stomping of tubes; more luminescent dye spilled across their clean deck.

"Chrissakes!" Albert bent over the railing, furious. "Fredy, getcher dumb ass up here and put yer dogs on a leash!"

Fredy flinched; almost lost footing. He shot a glare to be sure no one was snickering, straightened a dopey palm laurel nestled atop his black curls, and finally moved with the hangdog obedience of a conquered chieftain. After two failed attempts to vault the meter up to the ferry's deck, Fredy snapped fingers impatiently until the helmsman on his skiff gave a boost.

"Lookit that shit." Albert nodded at the dyed deck as the little squad leader shambled toward him.

Fredy took Albert's shoulder. "My friend, a word."

"Who's paying for that?" Albert thrust a finger at the puddles of liquid light. "That'll stain. The wood's ruined."

"My friend, my friend. A word."

"My friend, my friend. Eat shit."

Albert yanked away when Fredy tried to lead him bodily from the other bordies' earshot. Forced to clomp alone to the ship's bow, the squad leader gestured impotently for him to follow.

Fredy was humiliated. *Good.* Albert smirked.

Stretching lazily, he swaggered to the bow in his own good time. Broad-shouldered, strong-postured and—unlike many across the continent in such haggard times—*well nourished*. The estranged American territories were rife with famine, but for a shrewd smuggler there was peace and plenty.

Well, Albert thought, patting the holster at the small of his back, *maybe not peace.*

Leaning on the prow beside Fredy, he breathed in salty air. The Trans-Peninsula Canal waters were snaking south around them, high concrete walls cutting off all surrounding land. Carved ages ago to divert Gulf waters back into the North Atlantic, the main pump-churned channel was wide enough to sail fifty steamers abreast without touching bulkheads. Walls twenty feet tall from waterline to rampart.

Nothing to see. Florida was so damned flat.

Albert spied fronds fanning up from behind those walls, though, and grinned. Some flora couldn't survive the wild climatic shifts. But palms were resilient old gals.

Just like Lola. His eyes almost twinkled with anticipation. *So close I can almost feel her.*

"Shouldn't talk to me that way in front of the boys," Fredy interrupted the thought. "Looks bad."

Albert cocked an eyebrow. "Tellya what looks bad: pestering *me* like a common border jumper. I don't pay for the pleasure of yer company. Don't like ya that much, Freddo. Yer paid to keep the bordies off our goddamn backs."

The little latino looked wounded. "I am fun guy. Ask the boys. You ask. Life of the parties."

Albert studied the jumped-up imp. Likely from some Gulf Protectorate shithole: Tampa, the Mobile wetlands. Certainly not from the *real* New-East Bloc, mighty coalition of Midwest territories. The Great Lakes cities would melt his little mind. Living down here at the world's edge like a deranged little duke. "Defending the Bloc's fringe lands" by swindling refugees and Floridiot savages. Dealing with bordies made Albert nauseous.

"First off, Fredy, *y'ain't* fun," he scoffed, eyeing his palm crown. "Look in a mirror, ya creepy little fuck. Secondly, get everyone off my ship or there'll be a shitstorm."

"Must put on a show here and there, my friend," Fredy insisted. "Top brass is always curious: 'Why is not this boat or *that* boat searched? How come Fountain's ferry is never stopped?' Keeping my good name is not easy, you know. Or *cheap*."

Albert palmed his face. "Dumb sonuvabitch, tell me yer not trying to shake us down. See any Bloco sightseers aboard? That's cos our holds're overflowing with contraband insured by the *Trade Juntas*. Hearda them? Maybe ya seen some of the heads and hands they lop off enforcing the black-market."

Albert pushed closer, towering over the little man. "We got tungsten lining hiding us from yer scatterscans. But if this haul don't reach 'Chobee…if one of yer shitbirds down below, say, catches a peek and wants to impound us, wants a *taste*…" He frowned. "Let's just say there'll be some unruly customers in Okeechobee Bay. And the Juntas'll hear Fredy the dipshit bordie is responsible for their unhappiness. Okay?"

"Okay, my friend."

"Got me?"

"Got you, my friend."

"So, get these dickheads off my boat."

As the bordermen disembarked, Albert caught his dye-smearing buddy glaring up at him from the patrol skiff. A puggish, sunburned face beneath his state-of-the-art helmet quivered with rage.

Albert beamed back, casually bending to palm a cracked dye tube on his way to the starboard railing.

"Say, what's a fella gotta do to join the Bloc Bordies, anyway?"

"Fuck you care, smuggler?" the pug-faced borderman snorted. "Lookin' to enlist?"

Albert shrugged. "Curious, is all. Got rigid enlistment standards? Or they snag every inbred eunuch washout from Militia Academy?" *Little salt in the wound.* Famed Militiamen of the New-East American Bloc shat all over these clowns.

The bordie scowled, but seemed puzzled. "What's that word?"

"Standards? It's what yer ma gave up when she laid that hobo and made you."

Eyes narrowed. "Other word. *You-nick.*"

"Oh, that's Canuck, I think. Navy rank…kinda like ensign."

The man mouthed the funny word.

"Wait, no. I remember!" Albert called as their crafts parted ways. "It's a fat, dickless slave!" Reeling back, he hurled the tube across the water, biolume streaming like a comet tail. The tiny cylinder exploded against the borderman's chest plate, spurting radiant ink across his torso and face, spattering nearby comrades. Pugface hunched over the rail, spitting pure rainbow light overboard.

"Bon voyage, you guardians of the swamp!" Albert brandished two middle fingers at the departing skiff. "Go do what yer best at—shaking down glasshead gypsies and flood refugees!"

Watching bordermen flail in stark rage, Albert knew he'd be straight out murdered were they still aboard.

He was overcome with a sudden euphoria.

"That smart?" Remy sighed from behind him. "Eggin' on them vicious apes?"

"Remy old boy, in a drowning world *fulla* vicious apes," Albert chuckled as he flicked them off, "gotta savor them little joys."

"EFFORTS ARE underway by Nevadan Coastal Authority to curb the influx of Asian refugees into the California Annex…"

The woman sat enticingly—though quite weightlessly—across Albert's lap, affording an excellent view down her shirt. He wondered briefly if she was a *real* anchorwoman somewhere or a figment of neural programming, coming to the conclusion he didn't give a shit.

Peeling eyes away from cleavage, Albert readjusted on the ferry bench to focus on the AR newsfeed as they coasted down the Canal at full throttle. In midair behind the woman hovered mirages of ragtag refugee fleets. She batted long eyelashes, smirking as though the bulletin were for him and him alone:

"Everything from freighter flotillas to makeshift rafts have been encroaching steadily into Death Valley floodlands since the quakes last March which submerged swaths of East and Southeast Asia. NCA spokesman Robert Fitch had this to say about the humanitarian crisis…"

The busty anchor turned attention to an empty seat across the aisle on the ferry. A smartly dressed bureaucrat flickered into existence there, whiskers garishly oiled and braided in Great Basin fashion. If not for flashes of non-existent cameras strobing his face, killing the augmented reality illusion, Albert would never have guessed that his new "passengers" existed only in his mind's eye.

"I believe I speak for the whole Nevadan Commonwealth," the spokesman's mirage began, *"when I say we've the utmost sympathy. Their journey across the Pacific was surely perilous. But by settling in the region they're, frankly, infringing on Nevadan sovereignty. In light of recent calamities in our Cali territories, we haven't accommodations or…um…resources to grant asylum. Not with many of our own citizens displaced or unaccounted for. Deportation efforts must proceed."*

As the smiling blonde turned back to face Albert, something was at once jittery, arachnoid, about her movement. *"Fitch had no comment when asked about Indo-China's closed-door policy concerning safe harbor for ref—ref—you—j-j-jeeeeez—"* Her voice stuttered, squealed.

Albert shook his head. "Haze" computing was miraculous till you hit a deadzone and lost neural link. Measly *physical* reality dominating your senses once more. He winked the AR newsfeed completely off, having hardly digested a word. Woman and man sputtering out of existence like ghosts, back into the recesses of his fancy new neuraware implants.

The *Great* American West. Nothing but a half-savage nesting ground for the straitened, the starving, and the goddamn certifiable. They called it *the Outlands* now. A melting pot of caustic elements which burble and burn but willfully refuse to blend. Pacific refugees, drowned deserts, rampant slavery. Endless bloodshed between God knew how many regimes: Nevadans, Salt Lakers, Virgin Army remnants, Rocky slavers. Some *new* whack-job warlord rising from south of the old border calling herself "la Mami." All as remote and insignificant as anarchy breaking out on the moon.

RIP, Old Glory, Albert thought. *The Rift was always a matter of time.*

He laughed at himself now—pretending to care about the carving up of a dead republic. Only one "domestic affair" gave him sleepless nights. And her name was *Lola*.

"Heads up, Allie!" Remy called from the helm.

Albert looked up, seeing the bordie patrol skiff headed northbound the opposite direction. He wasn't worried but stood up anyway, touching the 'Backpack Cannon' holstered beneath his shirt to ensure the beastly silver revolver was secure. An archaic weapon by Bloc standards: noisy, kicked like a horse despite synthetic shock absorbers. But compact, lightweight, and its .460 magnum slugs could take a man to pieces. He'd only used it twice. *Three* times, technically, but that bandit had lived.

Have a helluva time raiding with one leg, though.

Bordies scowled as their skiff passed, activated chamelo armor giving the impression of disembodied faces hovering over the waterway. They didn't even decelerate. That goon Fredy had spread the word.

The massive portcullis of the Canal Brinkgate—last checkpoint before their world's end—raised without a hail, lifted seawater showering their deck as they passed beneath.

Spreading that goddamn stain, Albert thought, watching the bright biolume streak in the wet.

Beyond, the channel widened steadily over time. Concrete walls giving way to scrubland, scrubland gaping open into a vast ocean inlet. They banked slowly east to the shoreline, boat traffic dodging like schools of fish: sailboats, treadlecraft, windships, steamers, massive row-powered triremes and sleek solar cogs.

Once a massive landlocked lake, Okeechobee Bay now spilled feebly into the swollen Atlantic like a Titan yielding to a greater god. Unlike the rest of the Gulf of Mexico, Florida had been largely spared the onslaught of Great Gertie. But with a third of terrain already gobbled by the ocean, the peninsula had no room to gloat.

Albert gazed south. A salvage goldmine lost beneath those waves. Coral Springs. Lost Miami. It was said the old Four Seasons Tower jutted from the surface like one colossal headstone marking the grave of that drowned vacationland.

Just one long wet season now, he chuckled blackly. *Our Eternal Season.*

As a big rusted steamer chugged clear of their bearing, Albert spotted the port city. A barnacle-like sprawl of quays, storehouses, inns, taverns and seaside spectacle looking almost medieval except for holo'casts and sky-ads splashing it all in trendy neon hues. Okeechobee harbor was only decades old—cropping up along the former lakeside after hypercane Gertrude grazed—but it had a corroded majesty only seawater bestows. Like a scar worn proudly to prove you're not easily broken.

Albert gave Remy a finger-twirl and pointed to the

easternmost marinas.

The captain nodded through the cabin window with a scowl that said, "*I know my business, dipshit.*" Steering the ferry starboard.

They had solid connections in 'Chobee: Columbian coke, Brazilian genosplicers, glasshead meds and nanomeds, crazy new dope called *afterglo* from God-knew-where, fabrics from India, rare earth ore from Namibia, Zimbabwe…

But most crucial of all: illegally engineered foodstuffs from genebanks *all over*. Refab fruits, veggies, tubers, beans, grains, nuts, C-1 meat preserves—the works.

The almighty New-East Bloc declared unlicensed refabricated foods "hazardous to public health." Even in the face of famine, fearing those leftovers from bygone nutricide attacks. *Croakers.* The tiny cell-like assassins had once permeated domestic staples, perverting nutrients, rendering crops as inedible as styrofoam. But last reported attacks dated back to before the breakup of the Old States.

Few bad muffins and they wanna throw out the batch. The Bloc bastards wanted monopoly on the ultimate commodity: human diet. Their domain was largest in the former-US: from Iowa Enclave to PA, with protectorates dotting the drowned Gulf and East Coast Remnant; Militia and Border Guard outposts infesting the continent like cockroach nests. That shady *ECCo* corporation lavishing miraculous energy on the Bloc while so many in the world *still* scuffled over dried up petroleum wells. And supposedly this made them America's heir apparent.

There I go again—pretending to give a shit.

Albert beamed at the approaching port. Lola always

came down to meet him. She wasn't his only lover; trade took him all over. He knew lovelies from Pitts to Carolina to Bargeton drifting over the ruins of Orleans.

But Lola was on a level all her own. He'd first found her working in a dockside cathouse called *Wet Kittens* a decade back. Wouldn't have touched the other gals there with a ten-foot pole, but Lola shined like a jewel in that blighted hole. At first glance he'd known she wasn't just any Brazilian exile. She was a *Filha de Vênus*. Primo splice-job. One of those genetically engineered goddess-courtesans once enjoyed only by royalty and kingpins; last of the genic people to survive the South American massacres.

He'd had to pay and threaten, even name-dropping the dreaded Trade Juntas. In the end the pimps released her, and Albert set her up in a private bungalow beyond the grimy port city. Sometimes he convinced himself he'd done it out of charity. But deep down he knew he'd just wanted her perfect, taboo beauty all to himself. An exotic home away from home.

Which reminds me…

Shutting eyes, Albert re-established neural link to Haze. Tapping into the access field, reality ballooned around him. His consciousness amplified by quantum field interface, plunging into a sea of data as invisible and available as thought itself.

Nano-sensors told him it was 5:16 pm; sunset in two hours, forty-six minutes; temperature 94.7 degrees Fahrenheit; humidity 92 percent.

With his psyche "broadcasting" now at speeds faster than light, from particle to entangled particle, he could explore Pyramids or view the Louvre's drowned masterpieces, right there on deck, like a traveler through time. He could dogfight alien armadas while simultaneously reveling in AR orgies. Or opaque his own familiar senses altogether and steep himself in the sensual escapades of the Bloc's hottest simstars. See everything the celebs see, feel every tingle they feel.

Haze. Never get used to this shit.

He ignored it all, "dialing" the correct neuronal channel. Seconds later, a woman was flickering into existence before him on the deck. Slim, milky-skinned and pretty in her sweat shorts. Her silken red hair tied into an impromptu bun.

"Hey, Aud, baby," Albert said to his wife's mirage. "Arrived, safe and sound."

"Ah. Good." Her voice betrayed frustration. She blew a wisp of loose hair from her eyes.

"This neuraware crap making you queasy?" he laughed. "*You* wanted us to get rigged."

His wife had felt implantation crucial with his lengthy "business trips." He'd taken the horse pill just to get it over with. Audrey opted for intravenous infusion; hated pills.

"Nah, not that," she said. "Just Cloe. Y'know, she's doing that *thing* again."

"The cheek thing?" Albert grimaced.

Audrey Fountain slapped her thighs, exacerbated. "Won't swallow. Stores it in that damn cheek. Looks like some little dip-chewing laborer!"

"Lemme talk to her. Tap me into the living room holos." His daughter was much too young for Haze-rigging. The mind required greater development to tolerate the brainwave-amping substances of neuraware.

19

"Hang on..." Mildly relieved, Audrey fidgeted with unseen paraphernalia.

In moments, a bright-eyed, red-headed three-year-old materialized next to his wife on the ferry's deck. Her left cheek bulging.

"*Har, Darddy*," she sang, voice garbled by pulp.

"You rotten baby carrot," he laughed. "No sweet-talkin' *me*. No ma'am, not when yer driving Momma to the nuthouse. What's with the cheek, Clo?"

Her eyes narrowed into a scowl. "*Dorn't like dah taste.*"

"Folks out there would eat that mush straight from your little cheek and ask for seconds. Hungry, hungry folks. We talked about this, yeah?"

The child shrugged her little shoulders.

"Silent treatment, eh? Well, turn this over in that little red head: girls who waste food don't grow up big and strong. Know what happens? They shrivel up and turn into starfish. If daddies hate one thing, it's starfish girls. Boring to look at, too prickly to hug."

The girl blinked at him. Then chewed and gulped until the lump in her cheek receded.

"Thatta baby. We'll make a human girl outta you yet."

"When ya get *hooome*?" the child crooned. "Missya n'stuff."

"Well, I miss you and stuff, too. But gotta work so my girl can eat. Wanna healthy fat daughter, not a beanpole…"

The girl pursed her lips, deliberating.

He cocked an eyebrow at her. "Promise you'll chew and swallow for me? No more cheeky business?"

She nodded once. "Yup."

"Hold ya to it, baby carrot." He blew a kiss. "Beat it."

The girl beamed, blew a sloppy kiss and vanished. Albert sighed smugly.

"Any other catastrophes need a man's touch?"

Audrey laughed. "Allie, dear, eat shit."

"Don't gotta keep it crammed up in my cheek, do I?" He yawned suddenly. "Probably crash early. Meeting early tomorrow. Haze is patchy as hell down here. No local emitter, I guess." He thumped the heel of a palm against his temple futilely, as if this might clear spotty quantum reception. "I'll tap into a hotspot each day. Leave me a 'spatch if you need to."

"Alright, bigshot. *Beat it*." She smirked. "We love ya."

"Love ya."

As his wife faded, Albert looked to the seaport bathed in sunset's first buttery hues. There was a saying that two kinds of folks end up in 'Chobee Bay: "Those come *down* to drown their sorrows…and those bobbed *up* to the surface from Miami."

Love ya.

Albert didn't know which he qualified for, now or any of the countless times he'd come to the Bay. Was this sustaining a family…or escaping them?

Lola.

If you repeat something enough, does it turn meaningless? Or become an automatic function like a heartbeat?

Love-YA, love-YA. Lo-LA.

He spotted her now on the wharf. Her smile faint, but dazzling. Voluptuous body wrapped in a fitted lapis gown. Jet black hair streaming in the wind. Hands…

…draped over someone's shoulder?

21

Albert's jaw clenched. He shaded his eyes. What runty little sonuvabitch had an arm around *his* Lola?

She waved as the ferry swayed into port. What he saw stopped his heart; worse than any two-timing. *A boy.* Slender and graceful, skin nut-brown like Lola's. But those pale, avian eyes...Albert saw those every time he looked in a mirror.

The boy smiled.

Albert thought: *Fuck...me.*

FOR ALL OF ITS SQUALOR, Okeechobee Bay was home to the richest nightlife in the Gulf. Spoiled Bloc naysayers claimed this wasn't saying much for a drowned and devastated region. But Albert had always relished the Bay's artless charm...

Rundown cathouses across from exotic five-star restaurants; high-end hotels next to filthy splice-job burlesque shows; seedy dives beside posh kalypso clubs pulsing with sense-scrambling beats. Old waltzing with the new; angels with the demons.

A terminus zone technically free of jurisdiction, the Bay had become a nexus for black-market trade. And a melting pot of displaced cultures: expatriates from South America, Africa, Eurasia; even a few crystal-skinned *cybos* on their mysterious synthetic pilgrimages around the globe. Streets at night echoed with mingled melodies from bygone eras: accordion dueling with rakatak, sintir strumming beside guitar, the mournful whine of viola punctuated by thudding djembe drums or the soothing patter of Caribbean steel pans.

Right now those quaint motifs were nails on a chalkboard to Albert.

They were seated on the cantilevered terrace of Manduca Kwan, a snazzy Thai-Chilean fusion joint. The balcony sparsely lit by tiki flame, outshone by kaleidoscopes of holographic sky-ads overhead. Albert had stuffed his cannon into a cargo pocket so he could slouch and was drinking steadily, his fragrant dish of *khing charquican* steaming before him untouched. Across the table, Lola absently stirred her plate.

Albert watched the boy chow down between them, mind whirling with furious accusations, but refused to meet Lola's gaze. *Pulled her from the muck when she was sucking cocks for moldy biscuits. Here's how she repays me.*

Gorgeous goddamn kid, naturally. Mind drifting to his wife and daughter up in civilized Tallahassee, he clenched his teeth. Did Lola actually think she could blackmail him with some bastard?

The boy glanced from Lola to Albert, Albert to Lola, excusing himself for the restroom.

When the lovers were alone, Albert almost cursed her, meeting her eyes instead: jade gemstones. Lips full, but not collagen-plump or sham-spliced. Skin so silken, so damn-near poreless, it could only be the gift of genetic engineering. Body stunningly curvaceous, but not pornstar garish. Contours too bold and balanced for run-of-the-mill Homo sapiens. More like Greek sculpture crossbred with Egyptian Amarna art.

Filha de fucking Vênus.

Bred in vitro for maximum allure by Brazil's ousted genelords, the Pais Genéticos regime. Schooled in the sexual art, Muitos Gemidos (*The Many Moans*, he thought, *yeah, I've moaned plenty*). She enjoyed immunity to venereal infection and dramatically curbed cell-aging. Over eleven years, while Albert had creased and grayed, Lola stayed soft and nubile. Perhaps the only Filha to escape the bloody Gene Riots. Relic of a lost era. A living, breathing depiction of impossible beauty.

Despite his rage, Albert ached for her.

"How old is he?" he muttered.

"Raoul is almost ten now." Her trilling, sing-song accent stirred him against his best efforts. "*Belo*, no?"

"What's this kid doing here?"

Her brow furrowed prettily. "We could not very well leave him at dock."

"That's cute." Albert laughed joylessly. "Won't bother asking if he's mine. I can see it in his face plain enough." He glared into the verdant jewels of her eyes. "You've had him tucked away somewhere for a decade. Why pull the rabbit outta yer hat now?"

She blinked. "I have no hat."

"The boy," he hissed.

"Raoul," she corrected.

He set his glass down heavily.

"Don't care what his name is. Yer a *Filha*. Thought you couldn't, uh, y'know. Breed."

"I'm no mule, Alberto," she giggled. "What I say was, my kind can...how you say? *Steer* insemination."

His eyes widened. "So, you did this on purpose. Whattaya want, more money?"

"These things you say—you are being cruel," she observed calmly between bites. "Like you are possessed or something."

"Funny coming from a chick brewed in a vat." Slamming back, Albert folded his arms. "Yer either stupid, or scheming, or both. Wouldn't've done this otherwise. Dropping this kid on me like some crazy fucking stork—"

"Americans!" Lola cut in, laughing. "Rabbits and storks and hats and vats. Okie-dokie, easy-peasy!"

"Expressions."

She shook her head, tittering as she ate. "How you expect someone to know what you *mean* with this gibberish?"

"*Here's* what I'm saying: I'm visaed. Yer a spliced exile from some drowned Brazilian shithole. Know what those *Pura Raça* lunatics do to your kind?" *Stop now. Yer drunk.* He persisted: "I hear in New Sao Paolo they rip you all limb from limb, mount your heads on pikes. And I reckon they'd do just the same to any half-breed spawn of a Filha whore—"

He stopped abruptly. The boy had returned to the table side, gently smiling. Albert cleared his throat and slurped his old-fashioned, shaking his head. Lola pulled the boy close, her brilliant eyes lancing Albert.

"Don't hide viciousness, Alberto. I hide nothing from my son. Know why I had Raoul? I wanted him and your seed assisted. Simple. I never wished him to meet you—a man whose trade is lying. Who kills to protect his lies."

Albert snorted rancorously.

"Call me ungrateful," Lola went on serenely, "but you have never been called *boneca barata*. Cheap toy-doll. Never

25

been hunted down simply for *being*. I left Brazil to escape liars and killers…and found you. A liar, a killer. It is fine. This is life. Life does what life must, and Raoul and I have each other."

She brushed the boy's dark hair with a slender hand before continuing:

"But he wished to know what kind of man his pai is. As I say, I hide nothing from him. And now he knows."

The boy blinked at him, still smiling, before returning to his seat.

Albert was silent. How could he be anything else after such candor? His vision swam with spirits, but he'd swallowed her words in equal doses and they roiled in his belly.

He rubbed his temples, blew air through pursed lips, then rose from his seat and staggered to the restaurant balcony.

The street below coursed with humanity—all shapes, styles, colors—with here or there the glassy-headed shimmer of a cybo (*newfolk*, they dubbed themselves. *Pfft!*) spicing the human river with dashes of artificiality. A parade of fiesta performers made their way up the boulevard now, dancing in vibrant, flowing garments. Belting out a lilting Spanish tune somehow joyous *and* miserable.

Mexicans are experts at finding joy in despair, he thought, recalling the butchery of the Virgin Army's "holy crusade" across Sonora and into America just decades back.

Lola's hand touched his shoulder and he clasped the rail.

"This Bay's my home," she purred. "I've no dreams of being whisked away. You do things for me in your power; I do things for you in mine. It's a kind of love, no? Low-volt love. But who given an ounce has right to bitch?" She nuzzled his neck, words a hot breath: "Relax, you are not the love I want for *him*."

Albert turned to her now. She was his height; he'd always liked that. Neon light danced in her catlike eyes. She smiled, not unkindly. He glanced over his shoulder at her little brown adonis at the table going to town on his grub.

Love's just another currency, he thought. *Only one immune to inflation.*

Pinching Lola's chin, Albert meandered over to the boy. Watched him eat for several moments. Slow, methodical bites. Savoring each mouthful.

Most beautiful woman on earth. All she asks is a dash of sperm. Lousy deal for her, but one helluva con. He chuckled bleakly through his nose. The child glanced up at him.

"Good appetite." Albert slid his untouched plate over to the boy. "I like that."

THE VIBRATION WOKE HIM UP. Through the mattress beneath him: a bassy palpitation like a broken massage bed. The first thing Albert did was reach for his weapon on the night table. He'd learned long ago—cargo ransacked in a night raid—to distrust any minute disruption of sleep. Death rarely came knocking; it was a silent stalker. Flipping his bare feet over the side of the bed, he gripped the revolver two-handed.

The bedroom was empty, splashed in indigo shades of halflight. Beside him Lola slept, naked curves swaddled in bed sheets. But the shuddering persisted, and not just in bed. Feet placed on the hardwood floor, he felt it stronger. A quiet kettledrum thundering on and on, all throughout the bungalow.

Albert tiptoed naked across the room. The door creaked slightly as he opened it and crept out, taking cover behind a shelf. A light flickered just around the corner in their tiny kitchen. He took a deep breath to steady himself, thrusting the gun around the bend…

The boy glanced up from an old leather-bound book at the kitchen table, a soft peat lamp glowing beside him. He blinked at the gun.

"Christ," Albert sighed, lowered the gun. "The hell you doing out here?"

Raoul only turned back to his open book. After a moment, he replied in a dreamy, unaccented voice: "Thinking of a girl with hair like fire."

Albert squinted at him, confused by the response, but the tremors below held his attention. *Some pipeline?* He grabbed a nearby couch cushion to cover his shame and nodded at the boy's archaic reading material.

"Paper book, huh? Whatcha got?"

The boy said nothing, eyes dancing over the page.

Like staring into a funhouse mirror, Albert thought sourly. "Y'oughta respond when someone asks you a question. It's the thing to do."

Their twin eyes met now.

"It has no title." The boy grinned, bright-eyed. "But people used to call it The Swallowed World."

Albert blinked. He was no reader, but even *he'd* heard of it. Few decipherable words, but oodles of gibberish pictographs and arcane imagery. Most faiths called it the Apocrypha: an absorbing, if dubious, hoax tome. The Virgin Army had slammed it "Biblia del Infierno." *Hell's Bible.* Burned it wholesale during their American conquest.

No one knew who'd truly authored the work, but it had caused a bit of a stir years back. Quacks coming out of the woodwork to study it. Even inspired a cult declaring it an "encoded prophecy."

Occult horseshit to feed fools, he thought, but leaned in all the same. A cryptic full-page spread. He thought he saw some sort of beast-child donning gauntlets for eagle hunting or falconry; hair aflame, rising from a boiling sea. The sinister idol edged with unintelligible glyphs. But he blinked and the image seemed to lose coherence, like a disbanding cloud formation.

"Looks like a page-turner." Beginning to say something else, Albert nodded instead and beat a hasty retreat to the bedroom.

Lola was sitting up in bed when he returned.

"Doesn't that kid sleep?" He shut the door behind him before going for the nightstand, swapping his hand cannon for the quart of Scotch.

Lola stretched, sheets sliding from bare breasts. "He needs not so much as most."

"Lucky him." Albert poured two fingers, guzzling it. "He's a little *touched*, idn't he?"

"Raoul is gifted."

He snorted. "In what? Being a creepy little bastard?"

She was unamused. "He returns to our cuidador tomorrow for the rest of your visit. You know nothing of him. Do not speak of him."

Albert raised an eyebrow but shrugged. *Fair enough.* He poured another couple fingers, sipping slowly now. "Honestly, what's his score?"

"There is no *score.*" He sensed a slight hesitation before she said: "He feels things."

He gulped at his drink. "Don't we all."

"Not like him. He's what you call…empathic."

He squinted at her and chuckled. "Reads minds and shit?"

She laughed. "That's *telepathy*, Alberto—a cheap trick played by rig junkies. This is something truer."

"Lemme tell you something, and don't take this the wrong way…" He eyed her breasts as he sat on the bed's edge, sipping Scotch. "All parents wanna think their kid's something great. Especially those with rotten little shits or head cases. What makes Raoul so special?"

Her eyes glistened, hearing their son's name. "You really wish to go into this?"

"Sure. Plunge right in."

"Raoul…" she paused, "…*shares* deeply with others."

"Can't stand mystical bullshit. Clear language."

"New notions demand new language," she said. "He's unusually…observant. Makes him seem spooky and, uh, *aloofed* to many. In truth, his senses are elevated so sharply they are forming…a greater sense. Empatia, we call it."

"*Right.*" He downed the rest of his glass. "Well, that's a new one. I'll give you that. He babble in tongues, too?"

"You were an orphan at thirteen…"

Her accent had eerily dissolved—less like an actor breaking character than a voice abruptly flooded by well-springs of diction.

Albert gaped. His private edict was to never tell Lola personal history. "How'd—?"

"Your parents owned a bootleg refab farm," she continued, words flowing without pause for thought: "You saw them murdered for their property. The Partisans or one of the other southeast posses during the Landgrabs. Your father slain outright while your mother was violated. She fought like a panther, but they were many and she was one. How easily the many revoke the dignity of the one.

"Wandering alone for weeks, you were taken aboard a freebooter vessel for your knowledge of refab crops. You saw many lands and learned everything you knew about contraband. But you were beaten and sexually abused, bearing witness to countless other horrors I'll not mention…"

Her pupils, he noticed now, dilated and contracted wildly as she spoke.

"Brutality taught you tenacity and resilience. Escaping the freebooters, you made a name for yourself in the black market. Reimbursed some of your old captors for their tutelage. But revenge never refunds what's lost. You married your wife because she was young, shy, unworldly— everything the world stole from you. Your daughter's hair is red like hers. You always loved that she took after her moth—"

Albert's empty glass cracked on the floor as he lunged, cupping her mouth to shut her up. Face twisted in rage.

"Do not talk about them." He released her and sank back to the mattress, wide-eyed. "How'd…you do that?"

"Empatia," she said. "A talent Raoul inherited from *me*." Her voice grew softer now, accent reemerging. Head cocked, Lola studied Albert's expression. "Do not look so stunned, Alberto. It's not witchery. Just...*feeling* in higher-definition."

He shook his head. "Can't read a person like a fucking book. Ain't possible."

"No," she admitted. "It's funny to explain. Logic is, uh—how you say?—*weak footing*? Bends under pressure. Seeing, hearing, touching, smelling, tasting. Pieces of one faculty. As their limits expand, so does awareness. Patterns focus, hidden undercurrents. How things fit into the world." She broke away, chuckling in self-deprecation. "Talent wasted on a *whore*, no?"

He bit his lip, turned away. "Yer not a whore."

"I'm bred for it," Lola insisted. "Shackled. Even now in the midst of this lofty talk. Feel me..." She took his hand, moved it to the wetness between her thighs. Against all efforts, Albert felt himself stir. "*Pais Genéticos*," she almost spat the words.

Albert looked at her closely.

"You hate them. The old genelords."

She smiled slowly. "A slave should love her masters?"

"The mobs carried out...the killings. Genics had rights; you weren't slaves."

"Neither is a hobbled pack mule. That doesn't change its predicament." She caressed the length of her bare body, shuddering in unwelcome titillation. "Pais Genéticos made us beautiful and gifted...then handicapped us. *Crippled* our DNA with programmed impulses."

She slammed a clenched fist into the mattress to still her body. For the first time, Albert saw that within this sultry, serene creature a war was ever raging.

"They stumbled upon Empatia during such tamper-ings," she said, calmly now. "Hidden right there in human genes. Didn't know what they'd tapped. Used it for profit: breeding snoops, spies, sex servants who could read every tiny tell or desire. Ignored its true potential."

Albert was suddenly aware that the bungalow had stopped shaking. *Was it the plumbing? Or my own nerves?*

"Potential?" He squinted at her warily.

"Empatia unshackled." Slinking closer, Lola released a breath in his ear: "*Raoul.*"

Albert pulled away.

She laughed to dispel tension, and crawled toward him over the mattress; a tigress. "Think you're all so connected with your brain implants, your Haze networks. Yet a husband does not understand his wife. A wife does not know her husband."

Hands slid up Albert's chest, his shoulders, coaxing him back into bed.

Thinks I'm some stud horse for breeding freaks.

"If we could all do this thing," she crooned, "what a world that would be…"

He shoved her away feebly, but too late. Lost in her lips, her purring voice, those first spiraling hip motions which drove him so mad.

Hell with it.

He pulled her in as she mounted.

"A world without borders or chasms…" She was an undulating wave, engulfing him.

Let her pop out all the weirdos she wants. Changes nothing.

"No heartache or treachery…" Her body rolled upon him, eerily supple.

Tricks, all of it. I'm just in the throes of terrible beauty.

"The soul of a world born from nightmare."

As he reached climax, the truth struck him like a steam engine. He thought of his daughter, his *red-headed* Cloe. And Raoul's gently penetrating words:

"Thinking of a girl with hair like fire."

Albert shuddered, clasping Lola like a life raft— tenderly or savagely, he couldn't say. He'd never felt so defenseless. Not when his father had twitched in the dirt like a dying dog, not when his mother had screeched in violation, their home burning to ash. Not even when those sick freebooters had slipped into his ship cabin—drunk, chemmed up, cackling—to get their kicks.

Empatia…

These two had unraveled him, never lifting a finger.

THE RISING SUN was a molten glob igniting the east horizon. The cloudless, lavender sky strewn with a sliver of moon and the last stars fading fast before the sun's steady invasion.

Stars flee the blinding truth, like me, Albert waxed crap-poetic.

He was lounging against a pier post, eating an electric blue apple while the last of his haul was loaded onto the ferry. Royal pain in the ass, rising so early. But he couldn't trust this to anyone. Human nature: skimming off the top.

Couldn't have fallen back asleep anyway. Not after Lola's…*strangeness.* Albert had been bathed, dressed and nearly out the door when she had sung after him from a cocoon of bed sheets…

"So early, Alberto?"

Turning to look at her, he'd shrugged. "Business calls."

"Ah, business, yes." Shaking her head, she pointed to the packed bag under his arm. "Don't need Empatia to see you are filled of shit."

"I like being ready for anything."

She rose from the bed then, sheets falling. Stalking naked across the hardwood floor to study him. "I always see the scoundrel. But rarely the coward. How interesting."

"Oh, I'm not *that* interesting." Setting down his bag a moment, he touched fingers to temples in mock-ESP. "Go on, dissect me. Who'm I running from? My old squeeze? My by-blow? Personal demons?"

"You're not that interesting," she chuckled. "Some sharks suffocate if they stop too long. Momentum made them forget how to fill their own lungs."

"Another endangered fish. Whatta cliché I am." He retrieved his bag, looked at her, and shrugged again for want of words.

"No goodbyes," she said. "Stupid word which means nothing. Just admit when you've finished and thrown in your coat."

"*Towel.*" He pulled her close. "Always come back. You know that." Kissed her but she didn't reciprocate. "Am who I am, sweets. Nothing new under the sun, right?"

She had laughed at that, cackled. "All the funny things men recite to convince themselves they exist." Patting his cheek a little sadly. "Know what identity and ego are?

Safety nets. For those too spineless to take a plunge, find out what they are actually made of."

Glancing down at the water now, Albert awoke from his daydream. Something was off. The tide—it seemed awfully low. He frowned, tossed the core of his apple in. A tardy splash. Their hydraulic dock had been adjusted to make up for the meter drop in sea level, but dockers were still having a hell of a time packing the holds.

"Remy," Albert called to the ferryman.

"Allie," the dark little man grunted drolly from deck.

"What's the deal with…?" He gestured to the water.

Remy Dade gave the ocean a cursory glance, shrugged, turned back to Albert with half-lidded eyes. "Low tide?"

Albert snorted. *Ferrymen are no seamen.* "Sun's up and I don't want shit from bordie patrols. Got an ETD here?"

"Imports mostly loaded. Leave within the hour, ifya want." The man paused, squinting bawdily at Albert. "Short visit, eh?"

Albert glared back. "Something like that."

The man smirked innocently. "Some men drown they sorrows quicker than others."

Albert chuckled. "Back to work, asshole."

The man gave a mocking salute and went back to supervising the load.

Skimming a last time through his AR ledger interface, checking and cross-checking supply figures, Albert's ears began to ring. He winked off his neuraware rig. Wriggled a fingertip into each ear and yawned to dispel the sensation.

Strange pressure…

It was the hush that made him look up. Longshoremen all up and down the quay had dropped what they were doing, gawking, pointing out to the horizon. Albert followed their gazes, unsure what he was seeing at first.

It looked like…a mountain range risen from the sea's depths, but the notion was preposterous. His second thought was a cloud of smoke swelling inland from some offshore explosion. But its breadth spanned as far as he could see.

Hypnotized, he felt the shuddering on the dock beneath his feet, recalling the bungalow's tremors hours before. His blood ran cold.

"*Jesus…*" Albert gasped.

Remy looked up at him.

"Get off the ship." He was backing up the pier now. "Off the docks."

The ferryman screwed up his face. "Allie, the cargo—"

"Remy, it's a fucking *wave*."

Remy's jaw went slack. A cresting wall a hundred feet high, marbled white and steel blue. Albert yanked the dumbfounded captain up onto the pier. Without another word, both men turned and pounded up the dockside. Stumbling across the boardwalk and through an alley, threading between processions of Chavistas bearing their traditional effigy caskets down the lane, tearing through a bustling bazaar, batting away proffered goods, Seminole Revivalist crafts, silk pashminas. On and on.

Panic spread like pitch-black gossip. Darting eyes hunting for solace. A timid murmur throughout town punctuated by an occasional gasp, a wail. Those not utterly paralyzed by alarm jogging in aimless crisscrosses. And beneath it all: the stillness. Birds silent, air breezeless, ocean-song muzzled. Albert knew it well.

That eggshell calm before a massacre.

"Where we go, Allie?" Remy gasped.

Albert said nothing, did not look back. And Remy, saving his breath, tried his best to keep up. Sprinting north at full tilt back toward Lola's bungalow.

ALBERT DIDN'T WITNESS the megatsunami's collision. He'd seen enough death to know that only the doomed spectate. Nearly a mile on, he ignored Remy's futile play-by-play from several lagging paces behind: "Oh, hell!...It's...it's... Oh shit, Allie!...God!"

He heard the swell of water like freight engines thundering toward shore. Heard distant voices rise in a falsetto choir, a strangled melody less human than planetary howl of outrage. He heard the shattering of glass, splitting of wood, rupture of stone and gypcrete as buildings came unmoored from foundations. Like gypsy vessels flying sails of clotheslines and kilims. And the tinny clatter of pedicabs and ships caroming through streets like toys in a child's bath.

Albert panted, gasped, but never looked back.

The bungalow was yards ahead now. Even situated with the others upon its manmade hillock, it was not safe. Nothing was safe. *Size of that wave*. It might break upon the port city, but would engulf all. He tore up the bungalow walkway, bulling through the front door without even attempting to unlock it. It came halfway off its hinges.

"Lola!" he cried breathlessly into the main room. "Lo-*la*!"

The house was eerily silent against the turmoil from

the port city. A clock ticked. A baseboard creaked. The drawn curtains bathed the living room in soothing shades of mauve. And standing before the window, gazing quietly out toward the port…

"Where is she?" Albert demanded of the boy.

Raoul seemed bewitched by the outer maelstrom.

He grabbed the boy by the shoulders and shook him. "*Where the fuck is she*?!"

The child blinked. "Left for town ten minutes ago," he said softly, "to see a boat leave."

Albert's vision went white. The sound of gushing water brought him back. Spidery pink imprints were stamped on Raoul's flesh as he unclenched the boy's arms, turned toward the front door.

"Couldn't've gotten far," Albert mumbled, scrambling out into the yard.

Remy was just now cresting the hill, wheezing, the torrent of water closing fast. Albert waffled indecisively, finally turned to the house and began scaling its slatted face like a gecko. Reaching dormer windows of the inset second floor, he looked down to see the boy squinting up at him from the yard, clutching that worn book of his.

The Swallowed World.

Scrambling halfway down, Albert grabbed Raoul, swung him like a pendulum up onto his shoulder.

"Grab the slats," Albert barked, boosting Raoul's scrawny ass with the heel of his palm. The boy climbed nimbly, still clasping that damned book.

"Allie, help!" Remy cried, clinging to slats halfway up the house, losing footing. "Can't do it!"

"Well, I can't carry *you*, dumb bastard! Climb!"

Safely perched, man and boy braced heels against gutters to fight the steep roof slope. Just as Remy's head popped above the ledge, the wet wall collided. He screamed as water pinned him. The entire house shuddered. Windows downstairs smashed. The front door rent off its last hinge. Nightmare currents rattled through wood, plaster, roof shingle.

Albert and Raoul fumbled for solid purchase as brackish surf lashed their faces. Gushing up and over the roof's edge. With only head and one arm free, Remy was painfully restrained by the current, flailing for the other two. Strength of the tide knocking wind out of him, drowning him.

Albert was unwilling to compromise his footing, but the boy wedged his book safely between the slope and his backside. Then leaned forward and grabbed Remy's thrashing hand, with all his lean strength helping the man twist to a scrabbling position. Remy scurried up onto the slope, crumpling into a sodden heap.

A broken toilet beached upon the rooftop and a man straddling an errant palm trunk babbled in French as waters bashed him against their house. Hugging the splintered tree, he reached with one hand for purchase on their rooftop. Scrabbling and slipping and scrabbling again with the hopeless determination of an otter. But the currents dragged him on gibbering through the neighborhood with the rest of the city's flotsam like the river Styx unleashed.

"Think the roof'll hold," Albert reported mindlessly above the roar.

Remy had passed out. Raoul said nothing. Spitting out brine, man and boy leaned back against the slope, limbs splayed in snow-angel postures. Two demented mimes making light of all damnation.

Albert caught his first glimpse of Okeechobee—no longer a bay, but a raging oceanic annex strewn with debris, capsized ships, and palmettos bobbing like driftwood. Several buildings stood defiantly above the tide but many others were drifting aimlessly, or disintegrating like antacid tablets as currents ravaged flimsy frames. He thought he spotted the broken terrace of Manduca Kwan, but whatever it was foundered quickly beneath the waves.

"There she is!" the boy cried.

The world snapped into focus, Albert's eyes dancing over the water. "*Where?*"

The boy pointed but he'd already spotted her; could single her out anywhere. Fifty yards out, clinging to the highest panels of a solar harvester. Drenched, bleeding, boggle-eyed. Currents raged about Lola's lonely metal isle —a siren betrayed by her savage sea.

Albert cupped his hands: "*Lo-la!*"

The two castaways flapped arms rowdily to get her attention. It wasn't until flinching at a passing corpse that she chanced to spot them.

"C'mon!" Albert beckoned with an open hand. She saw the gesture, shook her head, gripped tighter. "Do it!" She couldn't hear, but he screamed anyway, waving her on. "Ride the current! We'll catch ya! *C'mon!*"

She looked at him, looked at the boy.

Then it happened. Albert felt it in his teeth before hearing it from the Bay. A timpani roll muffled beneath waves; gods upheaving, solid earth shrieking under physical duress. They covered ears and clenched jaws but it was in their bones. As drumming reached total cacophony, it resigned into a single baritone quivering in their gullets. Joined by a new sound. One he'd never heard before and wished never to hear again: a slurping so mindless and monstrous it made their ears pop.

The whole seaport of Okeechobee began a slow-motion concave plummet. Palm trees uprooting, toppling; fractured buildings overturning domino-style, plunging into boiling waters; the flooded city itself sucking inward like an unstopped tub. In and down. The earsplitting sound of terrestrial suction matched only by a roar of voices. So wildly sincere, so abrupt in finale, it could only be wholesale death.

Albert could only gawk, distrusting his eyes. He'd seen freebooters burn a village to the ground once. A whole Maine hamlet charred to nothing but husks. *But this...*

Hell Itself opened its muzzle to devour a city of men.

The bungalow creaked under strain, but held fast as currents violently shifted direction, reversing toward the sinkhole cavity of the Bay. Quenching its terrible thirst.

Albert looked at Lola, and she at him. Her mouth fell open, eyes like saucers. Retreating currents wrenching at her body.

A world without borders or chasms...

Later he couldn't recall if he'd shrieked for her or stayed composed. If she'd fought the currents or given herself to them as she had to so many unworthy johns. *To me.* He'd only remember Lola's divine form ripped away like a rag doll, currents reddening as she crashed against jags of stone and debris. Mangled, tumbling. A bold new humankind rent to pieces and fed to a hungry earth.

PART 2

RUPTURES

DAY PASSED into twilight and no one spoke. Either the shock was still too great, or nobody had any intelligible remarks about a bloodbath. Remy had roused sometime near noon and, for hours on end, the three of them quietly listened. Waiting to die. Now and again there was a distant human wail—some blood-curdling peal of terror or agony. And the planet groaned below like a babe squirming in nightmare. But nothing happened. Tension gave way to fatigue, even apathy.

Never mentions in scripture, Albert thought, *how boring the Apocalypse would be.*

Darkness fell. Quiet clockwork of the stars a cosmic formality mocking the ruin below. Flood level had retreated enough to reveal tips of shattered structures, bodies bobbing like gnarled apples in the slosh bucket of the Bay.

Albert glanced at the boy beside him. Raoul's attention fixed on the drowned city, holo'casts still aglow deep underwater like some inverted aurora in the depths.

After a few moments, the boy opened his book to a marked page. Peered at it.

He hadn't cried, which was eerie. The child Albert, hiding while his own mother was defiled and murdered, had nearly suffocated himself to smother his sobs. Raoul had watched Lola perish without so much as a whimper. What the hell kind of kid was this?

"What's her name?" Raoul broke their self-imposed silence, not looking up from his thick volume.

"Hm?" Albert grumbled after a moment. "*Who*?"

"Your little girl."

Looking closer, Albert noticed the boy's eyes—pupils dilating and contracting madly just as Lola's had the previous evening. He shuddered but did not reply.

"Her name begins with a *Kuh*," the boy murmured. "*Kuh*-something…"

"Whatever that is yer doing, don't do it in front of me," Albert muttered. "Like jerking off or taking a dump—do it alone if ya gotta do it."

Raoul squinted pensively, as if not hearing. "Her hair is so, *so* red."

"Goddamnit." Albert gripped the boy's arm. "Hear what I just said?"

Raoul was shaken, but nodded calmly. "You were making gross jokes. Because you're scared and don't know what to do."

He went back to "reading" as Albert released him.

"The hell you care about her? The…*little girl*?"

"She's cute. Like a mouse," Raoul laughed quietly. "Says and does funny little things. Spits her food into the trash when her mother's not looking. If I knew her, I'd show her why eating is good. It'd be so nice to have a sister."

Albert was too tired to be awed by the display. "She's *not* yer sister."

"You're my pai," the boy pointed out. "And she's your daughter."

"*My* daughter. Nothing to you," Albert snarled. "See how much you care about yer own kin. Watched her die and already forgot her, deranged little creep." Immediately, he regretted the words.

"I don't like what happened." Raoul looked up at Albert. "But water can't wash Mamãe away. I feel her." He lifted a hand, turned it about. "*Here*."

Albert winced. He tried to smile but sneered like a gargoyle. *Just keep nodding. Maybe another wave will hit now and end this fucking comedy.*

"So, Allie…" Remy's hoarse voice came from the other side of their roof, "who the hell this kid?"

Albert abandoned the child's piercing gaze, picking his way gingerly to where Remy was sprawled, crouching beside him. "Where we at?" he sighed. "Ferry ain't an option. Gotta be wrecked, capsized."

"Sunk," Remy agreed, distractedly pointing at Raoul's back. "Who this boy?"

"I dunno, Remy. Some brat," Albert sighed. "Forget the kid for a sec? Figure out how we're getting outta here?"

"What if *another* wave comin'?"

"You really don't know jack shit about the sea, do you? Tsunami waves strike at short intervals. Hour tops. It's been, like, twelve. *So*," he clapped his hands, "exit strategy?"

Remy exhaled tiredly but squirmed around like a sea otter to peer northward. Toward civilization. "Few miles north, they's a town on one of the Canal forks. Old 'Chobee. We get there, follow to the main channel, shoot for the Brinkgate."

"Bet bordies are going hog wild on the Canal," Albert groaned. "Can't we just get north of this floodwater? Find a vehicle, travel by land?"

Remy shook his head vigorously. "Nah. Gertie didn't drown Florida, but she do a number. Here to Orlando hardly nuthin' but marsh. Slow goin'. Lousy with malaria, them resurrected gatorbrids..." Remy snorted. "Shit, maybe even the Uncle hisself."

"Who?"

"Old Floridiot boogeyman tale. No story for kids." Remy glanced at Raoul, returning to the matter at hand: "We got nuthin' for bordies to impound no more anyhow."

"Right." Albert shook his head, thinking of all his profits lost beneath the waves. "So, we get to the Canal, flash our visas. Maybe score some evac back to the capital."

"And the boy?"

Albert raised an eyebrow. "What about him?"

"Bet he ain't visaed. Won't get through the Brinkgate without some finagling."

"Your point?"

Remy cocked his head at him. "I *know* you ain't thinkin' of leavin' him in this hellhole."

"I recall a certain captain abandoning a boatload of terrified Tex-Mexers fleeing the Blitz: *'Soto and his Virgin Army can keep 'em! Else them Rocky slavelords! Ain't on us!'* " Albert's best Remy impression. "What's this kid to you?"

Remy frowned, nodded toward Raoul. "He save my life. Ain't see *you* lift a finger."

"We're pouting, that it? Learn how to climb. They teach it at most juvey camps. Yer alive, suck it up." He paused. "And, no, we're not leaving the kid."

For awhile the two men said nothing, gazing into an abyss that was once a city.

"Hell, Allie," Remy gasped. "What on earth happen out there?"

He shrugged. "Can't dip into Haze to see what news-feeds are saying. Never seen anything like it. The city just…falling." Hands in pockets, he stood up to better view what the devastation had left for them. Slim pickens, but he spotted the upturned dome of a shattered gazebo floating in the moonlight like a giant water lily. Further out, some promising plasto road signs and broken awning rods.

"Shauna n' Manny won't never believe this shit," Remy said under his breath.

"Who now?"

"My wife. My boy."

All these years working together, never knew he has a family. He glanced a moment at Raoul. *Disaster's gotta way of exposing chinks in our armor.*

"No making sense of this shit," Albert muttered. "My dad, he was Christian. *Ish.* Not like those Virgin Army nuts; before all that. Came home from the Old State clashes and found God. Remember a kingdom in that Bible of his, wiped out for defiling God's angels or something." A flash of Lola plunging. His mother shrieking in the blaze of their smoldering home. "Consumed by fire. A few folks are allowed to escape as long as they *never look back*…"

He looked up, remembering he was speaking aloud. "Someone looks back, 'course. Gets frozen into a pile of salt. I thought it was bullshit. Punished for giving a damn? Dad didn't get it either—just hungry for *any* meaning after the Old Nation collapsed. 'It's a goddamn fable,' Ma finally said to stop that holy crap. 'About our staying power. Nothing personal. Fools point at fire and cry damnation. It's a medium of change. The doomed burn. The survivor learns to become like the *fire*. But only the guilty feel punished, because they can't take the hint.' "

"Goddamn, Allie." Remy said after a moment, shaking his head. "One time somethin' outta that mouth ain't hot air, you lay *this* doomsday Christo shit on me?"

For the first time in hours, Albert grinned. "We just survived something thousands couldn't. Questions later. Right now, we get the fuck out and don't look back."

Remy clapped his knees as he stood. "Now we speakin' the same language."

MUCH OF THE night had been spent scavenging components for a makeshift craft. The largest—the gazebo dome —was simplest to retrieve. Big enough to hold three, but made of a buoyant post-petrol composite. Even more light-weight than ever-popular plasto. Albert had lugged it back himself.

The crack in the hull was what caused delay. Remy plugged it with a caulk of foraged clay and vegetable matter, baked into a hardish sealant by lighter flame. Meanwhile, Albert and Raoul swam out to retrieve the "oars." On closer inspection, several of the painted plasto signs were visibly snapped by stress. But a few had remained intact along with a pair of long canopy rods perfect for poling away from collisions.

Aboard their quaint bowl-raft now, the rising sun found them well north. Most survivors they passed were caught up in private affairs. Three robed Shi'ites sat on the roof of a derelict diner, solemnly roasting fish on a handmade spit. A couple neo-Seminole *twospirits* in vibrant patchwork lugged bobbing corpses onto a knoll—the spliced-hermaphrodite shamans spitting bay leaves upon the dead to ward off fell spirits. A lone cybo in a passing canoe sat as still as a crystal statue until he (*She? It?*) spied Albert's craft, raised a glassy palm. Less plea for rescue than quiet salutation.

We are passengers of this world, and that's reason enough for hello.

Raoul waved back enthusiastically and the synthetic being smiled.

First person to hail them was on the bough of a cypress tree, blubbering words sounding German: "Bitte! Ich bin g-gestrandet! Bitte helfen sie m-mir runter! Bitte! *Bitte*!"

Albert and Remy ignored the man. Situated on either side of the bowl, they paddled steadily over muddy floodwater. Cross-legged in the center, Raoul craned his head to watch the hysterical man as they passed.

"He can't get down," the boy said.

"Shouldn'ta climbed up." Albert didn't turn. "Not stopping."

"He's worried about his family," Raoul persisted. "They live in the Bay."

"Fortune passes," Albert snapped. "Another peep and it might pass *you* overboard."

Raoul said nothing.

Remy glanced back at the child. "Kid speaks Kraut?"

"Nope." He recalled Lola's term: *Empatia*. "His family's fluent in New Age schmaltz."

Remy frowned. "Ain't hearda that tongue."

"Means *bullshit*, Rem."

The little man chortled. "You know his family?"

Albert clenched his teeth, mumbled: "*Knew.*"

They all fell silent, listening to the German's panic fade with distance. Albert thought he felt rumbling below, vibrating through water, but put it down to frayed nerves.

NEAR MIDDAY they reached Old 'Chobee. Downtown looked like a rice paddy, floodwater steeping low-lying buildings in deep sloughs of muck. Noting age and condition of structures—condemned motels, derelict bars, tumbledown pre-Rift suburbs forgotten by time—Albert thought the deluge an improvement.

A clinging heat swathed the two panting men as they rowed, garments stiff with salt and sweat. When they turned a corner onto the town's main sunken thoroughfare, Albert cursed. The column of refugee rafts, rowboats, pontoons and canoes cluttered the passage like pool toys. All lining up for the main attraction: the Trans-Peninsula Canal tributary bisecting the dinky city.

Remy snorted. "Looks like we ain't only ones with the bright idea to shag ass."

Albert grunted, studying all the ramshackle craft. "From the look of 'em, mostly native Floridiots without Bloc visa anyway." Albert stood on the bowl's lip to see farther, steadying himself upon Raoul. "There's gotta be an evac steamer up there, or sol-powered ship. They ain't paddling up Canal pump-currents on damn rowboats."

"Bordie checkpoint?"

"Could be." Albert shrugged. "Either way, we'll skip the take-a-number."

He nodded silently toward a swamped alleyway. Water shallow enough to pole, each man grabbed a long metal rod. Quietly propelling the craft toward the alley like a pair of gondoliers escaped from the doom of Venice. They cleared alley walls by mere feet, drifting through floating debris, and hung a right onto a backstreet adjacent to the main boulevard. The shortcut lead right up to the high wall of the Canal. On approach, they heard a bullhorn droning from the main thoroughfare and halted their bowl behind a brick building to listen.

"Documents in hand!" the voice called. "Have your documents *in hand* as you approach! Step aside if you do not have Bloc documentation! Everyone will be evacked in due course, but those with visas are first!"

Slipping into belly-deep water, Albert peeked around

the corner to the flooded main street. A line of sopping refugees filed from deserted boats blocks back all the way up to the first submerged steps of the Canal station.

A patrol skiff bobbed near the foot of the terminal, one borderman loosely manning its mounted gun. The bordie on the bullhorn was halfway down the stairs with a comrade checking documents, needling for bribes. But up on the top step, before the yawning terminal gate cut straight into the Canal wall, was a pint-sized bordie in activated chamelo. No mistaking the stupid frond-wreath atop tufts of black hair.

Albert crept back, reporting: "Our old friend."

"Shit. That fool Fredy?"

"Stay here." He handed his revolver to Remy, holster and all. "I'll book us on the Good Ship Lollipop."

"Don't." Releasing his book, the boy suddenly grappled Albert's forearm. "*Don't.*"

Albert frowned at Raoul, disengaging himself from clasping hands. *Couple hours together and he thinks it's a daddy-son picnic.*

"Don't want backup?" Remy unholstered the gun, studied it, shoved it back in.

"Stay with *him*." Albert motioned to Raoul. "I know how to handle Señor Shithead."

He sloshed off without another word.

"Freddo!" Albert called on approach. At the base of the steps, two bordies blocked his passage. He scoffed at their hard-ass expressions: "Yer boys need to work on their routine. It's good cop, bad cop. Not ugly cop, anal prolapsed cop."

"My friend, you are alive!" Fredy laughed, chamelo

cloning the sky's cerulean blue from this angle. "We are all the time meeting under funniest circumstances!"

"So it seems." Albert shoved his way through the guards. "You got more than a beached patrol skiff, I hope."

"Indeed, my friend, indeed!" Fredy cocked his thumb toward the Canal. "We've commandeered a *lovely* solar yacht on Bloc authority for purposes of evacuation."

"Hawking tickets, huh?" He stopped two steps below Fredy. "I need passage north."

"Interesting! Yes, many people is needing many things in such times. Sad that all cannot be fulfilled. Needs must be weighed to find the heaviest. They call this triad."

"*Triage*, you moron. Passage for three. How much?"

"I wish it was a matter of money," Fredy said. "Alas, *vitaler* concerns prevail. 'Asi los primeros seran postreros, y los postreros primeros…for many is called, but few is chosen!' "

"Woulda made a helluva Virgin Army prefect," Albert said. "Wanna keep quoting scripture, or tell me what'll grease those already greasy palms?"

Fredy folded his arms. "You are funny man, Albert. Talking to me this way. As if business between us is not on rocks. Like our joint venture is not sunk. When the king is discovering he has no clothes…he is not king no more. He is, um, the *nakedest* beggar."

Albert rubbed a temple. "Don't speak in metaphors. You'll hurt yerself." He gesticulated as if bartering with a simpleton. "What can *I*…give *you*…to get on yer *fucking boat*?"

When Fredy backhanded him, Albert lost balance. Tumbling down the Canal steps and splashing into murky water. Bordermen hooted in delight. The loudest from the mounted gun—the pug-faced bordie who'd painted Albert's deck with biolume dye.

"You may give me your tongue," Fredy spat. "You may lick shit off my boots. Lick them clean, fucking Bloco. Piss those fancy pants and beg for life. And *then* I decide if we shoot you now, or sacrifice you to the Uncle, let his gator-brids pick yer bones clean."

"The Trade Juntas'll hear of this." Albert spat blood. "*I'm* their Sunbelt Exchange contact. You'll hang from a palm tree, fucking yokel."

"My friend, the Sunbelt is lost. Or haven't you heard?" Head cocked, he beamed. "Guess there's no Haze access down here for rigged Blocos, but it's broadcasting all over the hotspots. Orders are to pull north of the Brinkgate, to Orlando. Florida is in a terrible palsy." He paced down the steps toward Albert. "I was born here, y'know. Little town called Lithia, near the Tampa bogs. A sad thing to know yer mama is ailing. I won't watch her die. I love her too much."

Fredy reeled back blithely, kicking Albert in the jaw. Toppling with a splash, blood filled Albert's mouth. A boot heel dug into his chest and he thrashed to keep head above water.

"But it's comforting," Fredy continued, "that one spoiled Bloco will keep vigil on Florida's death bed. After so much times biting my tongue while you *rape* her like a puta." He stomped hatefully now, pinning Albert underwater. Albert clutched at the boot without leverage. "We entomb you with her. Like the pharoahess she is, yes? Por mi mama."

The gunshot rang like a howitzer, echoing off buildings all down the boulevard. Refugees and bordies alike flinched. Paces away, belly-deep in water, Remy raised the hand cannon from warning-shot stance, leveling the revolver with Fredy's un-armored head.

"Let him up," he ordered.

"My friend," Fredy chuckled, releasing Albert just enough to lift his slobbering face from muck. "You are too much outgunned."

The bordies raised plasmic discharge rifles. Man on the skiff ratcheting his mounted ETC gun to punctuate.

"Yep." Remy never took eyes off his target. Thrusting forward, finger tensing on the trigger. "But I put one through yer eye, I die happy."

Fredy roared, a laugh edged with panic. "Albert, such loyal friends you have! We should all be so lucky."

Remy cocked the hammer. "He come up, or I put *you* down."

Fredy shook his head, still smiling, but raised his hands and lifted his boot. Albert splashed free, hacking up water, and immediately went for Fredy's sidearm. No old-school propellant weapon, but the new gausser. Bloc-issue magnetic-induction pistol. He ripped it from the holster, flipped the safety off, pressing it to Fredy's temple as he led him sloshing away to stand with Remy.

"Where's the kid?" he whispered, still coughing.

"Safe an' sound on that rooftop." Remy motioned to the two-story brick building.

Albert nodded. "Thanks for checking in."

"Thank the boy. He the one say you in danger. Say he

'feel you.' " He glanced Albert's way. "Whatta hell *that* about?"

"Discuss this later?" Albert said through clenched teeth.

"Friends!" Fredy laughed amiably, not relishing duty as human shield. "This stage in conflict is dubbed *stalemate*! A time for amigos to set aside disputes and nego-*sheee*——"

The final syllable seemed to hang in midair as Fredy's head came apart. Albert flinched as brain matter flecked his face. Baffled. *He* hadn't pulled the trigger. But feeling Fredy slump in his grip, it was clear someone had.

Behind rifle sights, most bordies looked equally puzzled until, finally, someone called:

"Peace 'n quiet!" The borderman on the skiff spat, sunburned face leering. "Thought the spic never'd shut up." Mounted gun still smoking, he flipped the monstrous weapon from semi- to full-auto, swiveling to sight his new targets.

Dropping the headless squad leader, Albert and Remy rushed for cover just as the bordie opened up on them. Great geysers of water fountaining as electrothermal rounds thudded at their heels. Hugging an alley wall, they squinted through squalls of plaster and shattered cinder block as plasma-propelled slugs gnawed away at the building's cover. Perforated like cheesecloth. A storm of debris. Albert was certain they were dead men until the mounted gun jammed and ceased. He heard Pugface curse, then heft and cock an assault rifle.

"Still breathin', smuggler?" the mutineer shouted, hopping down from the skiff into the water. "Got any more big words to teach me—like *you-nick*?"

Albert took the revolver from Remy, shoved it in his pocket. "I'll keep 'em busy. Get the kid off that roof."

Remy shook his head but complied, splashing off.

"I hope y'ain't dead yet. God *damn* I hope not. Just saw y'kill my commanding officer. That right, boys?" Pugface waded toward the alley from several meters away. The other bordies snickered, joining the hunt. "Got some words a' my own for ya. Big ones they teach us in Border Guard basic. Like *collateral damage. Summary execution*."

Albert blew out a ragged breath. "Technically ain't words! They're phrases, *eunuch*!"

Whipping around the corner, he squeezed off three recoilless shots from the gausser. The pistol thrummed with each pull, sonic booms reporting. The first was way off, erupting in open water, sending Fredy's corpse bobbing. The second cratered a foot diameter of solid concrete. The final shot caught one stalking borderman's raised arm, vaporizing polymer, meat and bone from the elbow down. He shrieked and bordies scattered to find cover, less emboldened with their prey fighting back. Then lit up his alley with a volley of gunfire.

Hell, this is it.

Albert cowered, building particles lashing his face.

When the barrage abruptly halted, he thought his eardrums had burst because a thunderous rumbling lingered. But listening to bordies retreat in panic, he knew something else was afoot.

Albert peeked around the corner, watching bordermen flee up the steps of the Canal terminal. A crowd of hysterical refugees rushing up to escape with them. The bordie rearguard screamed for them to disperse, firing salvos to slow their advance. Mowing down nearly a dozen on the steps before hightailing it through the terminal to their waiting ship. Glazed expressions of awe as they peered back down the main drag.

Albert turned to follow their gazes just as the wall of seawater hit him.

THERE WERE FLURRIES OF MOTION. Light shafting through voids without gravity. Shapes lingered long enough to form ink-spill collages before disbanding: broken tree limbs black in silhouette, watercraft twirling like playthings, eddies of rubble marked manmade by geometry, bodies twisted in fetal death poses. A crap artist's depiction of doomsday. And then a thick darkness…crowded with waiting forms…

A farmer shivved and shot in his greenhouse.

I always heard drowning was torture.

A woman gang-raped on her farmhouse porch.

But it's the fighting that hurts, idn't it?

A goddess's skull cracked upon a jut of stone.

Couple deep breaths of blackness and it's done.

A mother and daughter drowning in a rising tide.

Every pocket of air floods. Fill all up inside.

A boy…a son…orphaned by slain kin.

Kinda nice. Like yer not so empty anymore.

Albert came to, briny fluid burbling from his lips as someone pumped his chest. Shoving the man aside, he doubled over and retched up pints onto tarred roofing, purging enough for a full breath. His head pounded, throat and sinuses burning, but that breath was the sweetest thing he'd ever tasted.

He flopped onto his back, staring into clear blue sky. Two bleary forms looming over him. Rolling to cough, Albert spied currents raging beside the roof ledge.

"Howja find me?" he rasped.

"Kid again." Remy cocked a thumb at Raoul. "Got some eyes on him. Spot you pinned down by the Canal wall and I fish you out. Got savin' yer ass down to a science."

Albert squinted at the boy. Raoul rose, backing up to give space.

"Hey, kid…" he croaked. The boy looked at him. Albert tried to form words, but instead just nodded.

Raoul smirked vaguely and turned away. That book of his was lying open nearby. Obviously had been perusing it when hell broke loose.

Still wheezing, Albert sat up for better view of town, hanging feet over the ledge. Old 'Chobee was largely underwater, water slopping against the tall Canal wall. Most structures—save several two-stories like this brick pub—were good and drowned. But water level seemed to be subsiding as it coursed rapidly through the cleft of the Canal station, siphoned east on pump-currents to the distant Atlantic. He thought he spotted a few other survivors on faraway buildings or clinging to improvised rafts, but paid them no mind.

"What happened?" Albert whispered.

"Second wave y'swore weren't comin'?" Remy plunked down beside him. "Bitch came."

"Couldn't be." Albert shook his head. "Interval was too

long, unless…" He paused. "It was a *second tsunami* altogether."

"Weren't so bad as that first." Remy shrugged. "Maybe storm's just easin' down."

"Tsunamis ain't caused by storms." Albert sensed the earth moaning beneath them. "Something's happening. Fredy mentioned something."

Remy guffawed. "Y'mean asshole just try to kill you —that Fredy?"

Albert steepled fingers. "Bordies are retreating up to Orlando. He said it's all over newsfeeds. 'Florida's in a terrible palsy.' Gotta be some line he ripped from the report. Dumbass'd never come up with that himself."

"Guess I dumb, too. Whatta hell a *palsy*?"

"It's—uh, y'know. It's when…" Albert threw hands up. "Fuck if I know."

"A kind of paralysis," the boy said, "with involuntary tremors."

They both turned to gape at Raoul.

At the opposite ledge, the boy shrugged. "I read."

"Mouths a' babes," Remy murmured. "What it mean? Earthquakes?"

Albert frowned. "Florida's got no active fault lines or volcanoes I know of. No routine seismic activity. Tsunamis like this suggests…underwater landslides. Compromised sedimentary density. I dunno." Resting forehead in hands, he realized he was bleeding.

"How a *smuggler* know all this shit?"

Albert dabbed at his head with fingertips. *Flesh wound.* "My ma studied geology before the southern universities went kaput. Shifted to illegal refab farming with my dad to make a buck, but always called herself a 'rogue geologist' at heart."

Albert snorted in recollection.

Botanist dipshits, his mother had ranted one refab harvest in the family hothouse. *Dissecting lifeless crops to discover how the zealots spread nutricide vectors. Should've asked a geologist! Peeked into the goddamn ground everything grows on. Defoliating agents? Bah! Croakers were seeded* below. *Corrupting from within!*

That's when Albert glanced inattentively at the open book beside him. Images jumping out, grabbing him, like an ink-blot test. A city collapsing into a roiling sea. And an ugly splotch of ink which, like an optical illusion under unfocused analysis, took on familiar shape.

A *continent.* An America made alien by erasures. Gone was Baja California…gone was Panama, Costa Rica, Nicaragua…

Gone was the Florida Peninsula.

Corrupting from within. He rose with a start. It wasn't just nutricides troubling him. Those man-made atrocities had wreaked their havoc. For several seconds, Albert swore he saw Lola's "undercurrents." *The Calamities.* Climates shifting; weather patterns in chaos; glaciers melting; seas rising; geosphere warping from altered pressure; land eroding and buckling. A brief vision of a world inextricably linked. No plucking one strand without shaking the web.

"Florida's always been lousy with sinkholes," Albert said. "Lot of it rests on shitty limestone. But if we're seeing cave-ins the size of 'Chobee, we're talking…vast subsurface erosion."

"You sayin' what?" Remy gaped. "Whole damn peninsula might be comin' apart?"

Albert glanced at *The Swallowed World* again, but those apocalyptic images seemed to dissolve under scrutiny. Cryptic gobbledygook once more. Listening to the muffled bass of strained earth below, he murmured:

"I'm saying we need to get north of the Brinkgate. Collect our families, our belongings. And flee Florida's carcass for good."

Albert was starting to move when Remy grabbed his arm.

"Somethin' I needa confirm 'fore we carry on our merry quest," he whispered, glancing back at Raoul. The boy fixated on a fluttering insect. "That yer son there. Ain't he?"

Albert blew air through pursed lips. "Change anything if he is? Hm? Make it easier to ditch me and my baggage?"

Remy scowled.

"I gonna ditch you, I wouldn't save y'ass. *Twice*. I gotta son. Know what it all about." He began to turn, paused. "But a man stand up for what his. Or he disown it. Ain't no middle ground. Not in a sinkin' world."

Remy strode away to see to the boy.

IN LIEU OF RELIABLE TRANSPORT, they scaled the Canal wall. A natural slope of wreckage had amassed against the ramparts; a rejigging of debris (boat scraps, a sodden wood cupboard, dented steel barricades) completing a sort of rickety ladder.

They proceeded northwest along the rim; not a terribly cozy path—tributary concrete only a meter or so wide. But

Remy promised the walkway would widen to three meters at the main northbound channel. High up here, at least, was safer from secondary surges.

Albert took point, then Raoul, Remy pulling up the rear. Walking single file like shabby gymnasts braving a balance beam of dead gods. From this vantage they saw fever dream skylines of tropical ruin. Floodwater mirrorscapes of swamped scrub, rooftop archipelagos, lonely palms with fronds drooping like the manes of weeping mothers.

Albert shut eyes occasionally to attempt Haze link. Should've at least been a weak access field by now from the North Florida emitter. No use. Some sort of widespread electromagnetic interference.

Need to find a hotspot, reach Audrey, tell her to start packing.

He said little as he lead along the concrete lip, listening to Remy regale them with long-winded family anecdotes. Grateful for something to drown out his fears.

"My daddy, he from Trinidad. It don't really exist no more," Remy was saying. "Got us out while the gettin' good. Settle us briefly in Dominican Republic. Don't hardly exist no more neither. We move east to Haiti to escape them floods. And then leave Haiti when it swamped, too. End up near Baton Rouge." He chuckled. "Which *also* gone now. But this before Great Gertie come. Where I meet Shauna…"

"Your wife," Raoul said.

Remy nodded. "Gorgeous gal."

Albert glanced back to see Raoul's eyes doing their creepy thing and snorted. *Should I tell Remy he's wasting his breath? That the kid knows it all already?*

"Anyhow, I ask her on a date," Remy went on. "All nervous. Ain't talk to American girls hardly. But she agree. So, we eatin'. And I talkin' too much cos I nervous as hell. Ramblin' about my life story. All them places I lived. And she stop me. 'Damn, Remy,' she say, 'you sink *every* home you had, or just them you don't like?' This a funny gal. Boy, I laugh!"

Raoul laughed.

"Ain't done, though, ain't done. See, by and by, we have Manny—"

"Your son."

Remy nodded. "Gorgeous boy. Take after his moms. Manny five or six then. Ask me about my daddy, where we come from. So, I start tellin' him all the different places I lived. And he stop me: 'Daddy, didn't you like none a' your homes?' And I say: 'Yes, I did.' And he scrunch up his little face: 'Then why you *sink* 'em all?' "

Remy and the boy cracked up. Albert couldn't resist a smirk.

"Thought Shauna put him up to it. Play joke on me." He tittered. "Nope. Thought of it hisself. Smart boy. Like you."

"Wish I could meet him," Raoul said.

Remy grunted. "Yeah? We just see, huh? Future fulla surprises."

The boy turned, glancing strangely at the dark man. Almost dejectedly.

Either seeing he'd overstepped or thinking of his distant family, Remy fell silent.

Just what I need, Remy, Albert fumed. *Fill his head with hopes.*

They reached the main northbound channel just before sunset. From up here, the immense Canal intersection was a sight to behold: the opposite wall of the main channel four football fields away over a raging manmade river of rerouted seawater. Albert felt like a microbe watching lifeblood pump through the arteries of a sleeping leviathan.

A grated catwalk over the tributary mouth permitted safe passage to the east wall of the massive channel. Heading due north now, they breathed a sigh of relief as their parapet widened enough for all to walk comfortably abreast. Breathing room to spare. To their left, the flowing Canal; to their right, the vast span of eastern marshes. When the sun had dipped below the horizon—world alive with starlight and frog chorus and the zip of orbiting mosquitoes—Albert gave Remy a look.

As the captain fell back several paces, he turned to Raoul.

"Say, um, kid." The boy looked up at Albert. "Back there. In the town…" He blew air through closed lips. "I see now. You tried to warn me with that *thing* you do. You felt the danger…before we were even in danger."

"I felt the men who were lying to the people," Raoul said. "The men in uniforms. Didn't think they had rules anymore. Wanted to cheat and desert them all."

Albert nodded casually but inside he quaked. "Don't get how you do it, but I can't deny it now. In fact, seems it might help get us safely outta this place. So, what I said before…about not doing it front of me? Forget that. You get a feeling about a situation, a person, speak up."

"I won't do it to hurt people."

Albert narrowed eyes at him. "Not asking you to hurt people. I'm asking you to keep others from hurting us. Can you do that?"

The boy nodded. "Yes, Pai."

Albert winced at the word. "Don't call me that, huh? How 'bout Mr. Fountain?" *Kinda formal, asshole.* "Or Albert. Allie."

"Yes, Mr. Fountain." The boy hugged the volume to his chest now as he walked.

"Why you carry that book around?" Albert said uneasily.

"It was Mamãe's."

Albert nodded slowly. "The say ol' Soto had most destroyed. And all electronic copies were unstable for some reason, data corrupted. Where'd *she* get a copy?"

"A strange man in Brazil. When she was a girl." The boy seemed to hug it more fiercely; a precious family heirloom.

"Yer telling me you can actually read that shit?"

Raoul shook his head. "But sometimes when I look at it a certain way…it's like I *see* things. Stories in the pictures."

The whole thing gave Albert the willies. He dropped it. *Let the kid have his spooky memento.* They walked awhile in silence, Albert not knowing what to discuss with a freak-child. After a long interval, staring down at his feet, he chuckled.

"Hey," Albert said. "Tell me what I'm thinking *right now.*"

"Can't read thoughts." Raoul frowned at him. "Just… soak up feelings through feelings."

Is there a difference? Albert thought. "Alright, whatever.

Tell me what I'm *feeling* now. Walk me through it slow so I can see how it works."

"Sure?"

"Shoot."

"You're scared of being spotted," the boy reported. "Try to look calm. But jerky eye movement, tense shoulders, stooped pose, stepping like the ground is loose. A lime smell like panic. You feel exposed up here. You worry about your family. Close your eyes occasionally to use your implants. When you can't get through, you grit teeth, make a tiny noise in your throat. Fidgeting, knuckles white. An anxious vinegary scent. We haven't eaten all day. The headache makes your brow scrunch. A sweet smell to your sweat. You are very hungry. You squirm when your stomach growls because you think it's embarrassing." He paused for a second. "There are lots of things, but what you wanted me to guess, what you found funny, is that we both drag our heels when we walk."

"*Jee*-sus Christ!" Albert howled with laughter. *And only,* he knew, *a layman's glimpse of the full ability.*

Raoul laughed abashedly.

"What so funny up there?" Remy called.

"Alright, do Remy now," Albert whispered to the boy.

"I don't like doing this. Showing off. Makes me feel weird."

"Just do Remy, do Remy," Albert insisted. "Don't gotta do the whole spiel. Just tell me something he's feeling deep down."

The boy blinked a few seconds, as if cycling through answers. Finally, he chuckled and sighed. "Remy has to go to the bathroom. Really bad."

Albert wheezed. "One or two?"

"Both. He wants to stop at those overhanging trees up ahead. So he can...*use* their leaves." Man and boy fell silent with anticipation as the tree limbs in question neared.

"Hey, uh, ya'll keep goin' a-ways. Business."

Albert and Raoul exploded with laughter, doubling over as they walked on to give him room. For the life of him, Remy couldn't figure out what was funny.

THEY SAW the man in the first gunmetal glow of day.

They had camped high atop the wall for a few hours in the dead of night to catch some shut-eye. Splayed out on concrete. But then the rains had come. First drizzling, then whipping without warning in vicious tropical squalls. Curse of the Calamities. *Gertie's Gift*, locals called it. Without shelter of any kind, they had little choice but to rise and continue north, hoping for the freakish storm to end. The crack of thunder and ceaseless flutter-flare of heat lightning said such hope was fruitless.

The downpour was still torrential when the man called up to them through a dreary dawn. Albert couldn't make out his words through the spatter of rain and roll of thunder, but could tell by the hallooing tone that it was no threat or cry for help.

The man was on the raised doorstep of a stilt house amidst a lonesome grove, deep foundation piles elevating his whole plasto structure safely above flood level. Buttery light glowed in windows and poured from the open door where he waved. Solar cells atop the roof clearly still harvesting abundant juice even through cloud cover.

"Don't like it," Albert grunted, flat on his belly.

"You like *this* better?" Remy called from opposite Raoul, gesturing to the sky just as lightning lanced a nearby lightning array, thunder boomed.

The boy between them flinched.

We're liable to get struck. "Whatcha think, kid?" Albert looked at Raoul.

The drenched boy was squinting at the stilt house thirty yards out. "He's telling us to come take shelter. Says this tree is like a natural ladder." Raoul gestured to the old mulberry hugging the Canal wall nearby.

"But howya *feel* about it?" He gave the boy a knowing look.

"Allie," Remy scoffed, "why you pesterin' the poor kid?"

Albert ignored him, watched the boy. Raoul looked miserable, fighting to keep his mother's book dry through the storm's onslaught.

"Alright," Albert sighed. "Let's climb down."

The tree was sodden and slick. But its limbs had firm, abundant foot holds. The three of them achieved the descent carefully but quickly. Albert kept the book above water for the boy as they swam for the staircase of the lofty dwelling. He reached the landing first, found his footing, felt for his gun, and glared up at the man at the top of the steps.

"Wet enough for ya?" the man said pleasantly.

"This yer house?"

"She is indeed."

"You offering shelter, or were we mistaken?"

"Wouldn'ta called ya otherwise," said the man. He studied the three soaked souls at the base of the flooded stairs. Waving them up as he leaned into the door, opening it wider. "Come get dry. There's grub, if yer hungry."

Albert studied the man a moment. Mid-forties by the look of him, hair and beard hoary but neat. Pale eyes weary, but kind.

"Wouldn't happen to have a Haze hotspot, wouldja?"

The man smiled. "Today's yer lucky day."

THERE WAS stew simmering on the stovetop at the kitchen island. It smelled mostly of onion and barley with a faint hint of something meat-like. Nothing C-1 refabricated, Albert noted. Likely chunks of aidmeat: the imperishable nutrient steak the Bloc engineered to dole out in famine lines. Nonetheless, the scent set his mouth salivating.

Their host, named Miles, set three bowls steaming on the countertop. Mounting a stool, Remy immediately dug in. Albert ached to do likewise, but other concerns prevailed.

"So, this hotspot of yours...?" he pressed. Such hubs opened local "portals" into the Haze nexus, accessible via compatible device or—in his case—implant. He didn't know how it worked so far from true Haze emitter fields (some egghead mumbo-jumbo about quantum mechanics) and he didn't care. All that mattered was getting access to those roiling data seas.

"Ah, yeah, " Miles said, pouring them tall cups of

filtered water. "Hub's on the upper floor. I'll go power her up in a sec. But eat something. Look liable to collapse."

Albert was anxious to contact Audrey but nodded in agreement, exhaustion hitting him now. He spooned his bowl, took a bite. The zestiness masked the bitter tang of the spongy aidmeat quite well. "So, where are we?"

"Near Lorida," Miles said. "Where ya'll comin' from?"

"The Bay," Albert said between bites.

"I've heard stories," the man perked up, disturbed but hungry for details. "It's true, then? Did…any others make it out?"

"You know more than us." Albert glanced up. "What with your hotspot."

Miles nodded slowly, distantly, chewing his lip.

About then, Albert realized Raoul hadn't touched his food. Slouched in his seat, eyes shut. He rattled the boy's bowl against the countertop until he opened his eyes.

"Where ya'll headin'?" Miles said. "North?"

"That's the plan."

"Hm," the man grunted. "Gotta boat?"

Fulla questions. "Yep," he lied. "Little dinghy we tied off at a jetty down the Canal a-ways. No canopy, that's why we were out looking for shelter." Albert studied Miles now. "Might think about shoving off yourself. Got yer own boat, right? With a marsh house like this?"

"Whatever ya do, don't stray northeast. That's where the Uncle roams." Miles was either preoccupied or ignoring the pointed question.

Albert snorted. "Third guy in twenty-four hours trying to haunt me with local legends." He glanced at Remy, who looked drowsy now that he'd scarfed down his meal. "Floridians are a spooky lot."

Miles chuckled. "Down here...the mind boils. Y'ask me, place was never meant for men. Brits tried. Spaniards *twice*. Then Americans took their stab. Came for fountains of youth, freedom from slavery, seaside paradise. Found humidity, high tides, hurricanes. And tropical monsters." Miles paused, smiling wanly. "Never seen Uncle's signs myself. But hear strange things. Families missing. Villages found half-eaten by gatorbrids..."

Looking at Raoul, he clammed up.

"Anyhow, I wouldn't be caught dead near ol' Kissimmee forest."

Lightning flashed.

Albert glanced at Raoul. Saw panic now on the boy's face. *Is it the ghost stories...or is he getting a feeling?* Albert stopped eating. "What's this Uncle supposed to be anyway?"

"Madman, I guess. But that'd imply he's human. Human cares. Human wants," Miles was trying to sound cheeky, but an odd quaver shook his voice. "They say when folks're weakest, that's when Uncle comes. Appearing from them old woods, riding a gatorbrid's back. He's more like *them*, I guess. An extinct predator reborn."

"*Spine-tingling*," Albert scoffed, but felt a sudden vertigo. Raoul looked up at him, irises in chaos. *Shit, something's up.* "Say, Miles. About that hotspot..."

"Yeah, sorry. Flappin' my gums. I'll crank her up directly." Miles laughed absentmindedly as he walked from the room.

"This isn't his house," the boy whispered. "He did something to the food."

Albert glared into his bowl. Glanced at Remy, teetering now on his stool in fatigue. Albert put down his spoon.

"He wants to rob us," the boy whispered. "And leave."

Albert blinked at Raoul. A second later, Miles paced back into the room, hands behind his back. Albert drew his revolver immediately, leveled it with the man's face.

"Drop it," he commanded. "Whatever you got, you drop it." He cocked the hammer. Vision swimming slightly. "Or I'm redecorating."

Thunder rolled.

The man froze in the kitchen, wide eyes dancing, chest pumping rapidly. Slowly he raised a steel-tipped baton from behind his back with three cautious fingers. Let it clatter on the tile. Then did the same with a hunting knife, showing Albert empty palms afterwards.

"That it?" Albert asked.

"Wouldn'ta hurt ya," the man said, breathless. "Ain't like that. Place's stocked with food for ya anyhow."

Albert ignored the excuses. "Knife and cudgel…that all ya got?"

The man nodded.

"You really got a hotspot, or was that bullshit too?"

He shook his head. "I'm sorry. Didn't know what kind ya'll were. If you were the Uncle's or what. Got desperate need for a boat." He quivered, eyes mad. "This whole damn peninsula's haunted. *Need* to get outta here, get home. They're out there. In the bogs. *Everywhere*. All this disorder…it's a smorgasbord to *them*."

Albert lowered the revolver slightly, scratching his scalp with the other hand.

The man's gaze dropped to his feet. "I am so sorry —I am."

"Right." Albert nodded. "Heardja the first time. Yer forgiven."

Raoul screamed: "*No!*"

The blast was deafening in the enclosed space. In the muzzle flash, Albert watched the shot take the man full in the torso, rip through his chest cavity, flecking the cabinets behind him. He was dead before hitting the ground.

Remy's eyes snapped open. Falling off his stool, he scrabbled away from the carnage. "Whatta hell *happenin'*?!"

Raoul pressed hands to ears, clenching eyes shut. "You didn't have to *do* that!"

"Shut up," Albert sighed. "Man wanted to gut us."

"He was just afraid."

"Seen what men are capable of when they're afraid." Albert flicked the cylinder open, thumbed out the huge spent shell, filled the empty chamber with a fresh one from his belt pouch, flicked the cylinder closed. "Woulda played penitent and slit our throats on the way out."

"He's not a killer," Raoul insisted, gazing down at the dead man. Irises going. "He lives in Birmingham. A volunteer medic since the Virgin Army purges. Treating villages of scourged children. The cruelty he saw…damaged him. He adopted a war orphan. His *daughter*. She has bad lungs. Medications pricey in Bloc territories. He travels to Okeechobee to barter. Stranded here on his way back. Chased by something out in the woods. Only wanted to get medicine back to his daughter before she—"

"Fucking stop that!" Albert grabbed the boy by the collar and yanked him close. "I don't care who he is, where he's from. Any man draws on me digs his own goddamn grave."

The boy's eyes met his, stopped dilating.

From the floor, Remy looked on speechlessly.

"Now let's make one thing crystal clear, and I know yer sharp enough to understand," Albert said, calmer now. "If I can get you past the border, for yer mother's sake, I will. But that's it. You may be my blood…but y'ain't mine. Never were. And if you ever question me again, I'll ditch you in the next bog. Do you get me?"

Suddenly, eerily, Raoul's distress faded. Fists dropping from ears. "Yes, Mr. Fountain."

Albert dropped the boy coldly, snatched the dead man's hunting knife from the ground. "We move as soon as the storm dies." He turned to Remy, still huddled on the ground. "Rem, you've been drugged. Help me search the place for supplies, then sleep that shit off."

Albert paced out of the room, began rifling angrily through a bedroom closet.

Remy entered, dazed, touching Albert's shoulder. "Allie, damn. Go easy. He a boy."

"No, he's not!" Albert ripped his arm away. "He's an *empath*. A goddamn Genéticos-brewed freak like his mother. Right now he's rummaging through us like a kid in a candy shop. So be careful what you *feel*, Remy. Got no secrets around him."

Remy seemed startled by the revelation. Unnerved. But clenched his jaw. "Whatever he is, he still a child. *Yers*."

He grabbed Remy viciously by the collar, sneered:

"Already gotta family to care for. When's last time you paid yers a visit? Hm? Sometime between whorehouse sprees, kalypso benders? No more lectures, Father of the Year. Help me find supplies, or fuck off and die in this swamp."

Albert shoved him away. Remy tensed, set to attack, but his face went suddenly blank. He eyed Albert like a stranger, turned and walked away. Moments later, Albert heard him going through cabinets in the kitchen. *Let him sulk.*

He found a rucksack in the bedroom likely belonging to the dead man. Inside he found inhalers, nebulizers, vials labeled *ipratropium* and *albuterol*. He pushed the sack aside, continued scouring the house. But was unable to shake the image of a sick girl in Alabama territory who looked kind of like his Cloe. Whose father would never come home.

THEY AWOKE TO MORE TREMORS, worse than before. Rattling up through the stilt house's pilings. Immediately, they collected their goods and waded across the water to their climbing tree.

Albert told himself it was stupid to stick around as long as they had but, in truth, he needed rest. They *all* did. They held their two rucksacks up high to keep them dry, handing them up the tree assembly line-style. Remy up to Raoul on a middle branch, Raoul passing to Albert higher up, Albert tossing sacks up onto the Canal wall.

The house had been well-stocked with refab goods. Whoever had truly lived there must have fled. Only someone hauling ass would leave so much precious foodstuff behind. Albert and Remy had taken all the grub and water they could carry along with first aid supplies: bandages, tape, and antiseptics.

The three hiked in silence, conversation seeming off-key after the morning's grim events. The sky was clearing now and the sun peeked through a thin smear of altocumulus clouds, bathing the mid-morn in cheerful light. But the land around them was a desolation and the ground still shook beneath their feet.

Albert paced well ahead of the other two. After awhile, he listened as Remy tried to teach Raoul some game, but the boy was deeply withdrawn.

"Clench hands together like *that*," Remy whispered. "A ball. There y'go."

"What now?"

"Tap y'own chin, now tap *my* hands. Back'n'forth. And sing, '*Bubblegum, bubblegum, in a dish. How many pieces do ya wish*?' "

"Why?"

"It's, uh, just the words you sposed to say."

"You don't know why." The boy paused glumly. "It's just a game your son used to play."

"Um…" Remy was clearly spooked by the bold display. "Well, yeah."

"Thanks, Mr. Dade. I don't want to play."

They both fell silent.

Based on vicinity to the town of Lorida, Albert judged they'd reach the Brinkgate before nightfall. A straight shot —that was the easy part. What troubled him was what they'd find when they got there. They couldn't hike the wall forever. Would the great gate be opened to the unvisaed masses with evac transports? Would it be locked and deserted by the retreating Border Guard...everyone south of the Brink left to brave perilous marshlands, or drown?

Albert couldn't guess. But one bad omen soon presented itself. He watched the steady churn of Canal pump-currents stagnate to a sluggish, dying flow. He pointed to the anomaly with a cynical finger.

Remy gaped. "The sea pumps been turned off?"

"Or destroyed." Albert listened to terra firma grumble.

"That ain't good."

Understatement of the century, Albert thought. Ocean levels rising. No Gulf pumps redistributing post-Gertie run-off to the deeper Atlantic. The west coast, Tampa to Tallahassee, would be inundated in months. More tonnage on an already strained crust...

And then our Eternal Season truly begins.

They stopped to eat in early afternoon, plopping down in the half-shade of a Canal structural girder and picnicking right on the concrete. Remy, still sour with Albert, collected his food and stood while eating. Pacing the ledge to peer down into listless Canal flow, leaving the others to their own devices. Raoul laid out his book carefully to dry in the sun while he ate. Albert watched him gobble every inch of his rations, down to stone and core.

At least he's got that appetite, he thought.

"Can I ask you something?" the boy said suddenly to Albert, watching Remy toss the core of his apple down into the Canal.

"You just did," Albert muttered. "But go ahead."

"What kind of man was your pai?"

"*My* dad?" Albert chuckled bleakly. "Just use yer little peeping tom power and get to know him yerself."

The boy looked up now. "He's passed. Too far removed. I can't feel him like that. Only *your* impressions of him."

Albert squinted at the boy. "So, read my feelings and be done with it."

Raoul shrugged. "A person's voice is nice. When it's not lying."

Albert grit teeth at that remark, but calmed himself. "My dad was quiet. Goofy. Liked tending crops, magic tricks, stories. Never said much about himself. My ma said there wasn't much left when the Georgia Legion shipped him home after the Memphis Massacre. Had the shakes. She brought me up mostly."

"What was she like?"

"A pill. Educated. Smarter than most folks after the school systems broke down. But a hard gal." He closed his eyes and, for the millionth time, heard her final defiant cries. "She grew up in a hard time."

"The Rift."

"That's right. Heard about the Great Rift?"

"Some in books. How the old country split apart. Because of the Calamities and starving. Goods and fuels. Religions and armies and diseases and skin colors and… there's too much to follow." Raoul rested his chin on a knee. "Seems like they wanted more reasons."

Albert grunted. "Fair assessment."

"Was it scary to her?"

"Scary to many, I imagine. No society admits it's losing its mind." Albert was lost in a fog of memory. "Used to tell me, 'Al, you listen up,' she'd say, 'Mankind isn't as good as its word. They drop the act when they see there's no audience. Oaths break and aren't worth swearing. Nations fall and aren't worth making.' Fiery woman."

"She didn't like the America?"

He thought about that.

"I think to her it was a promise broken long before it was made."

The boy nodded, growing quiet.

"Can I ask *you* a question?" Albert said.

"You just did. But go ahead."

Albert couldn't help smiling. *Can you inherit smart-assery?* "This thing you can do. This...*Empatia*. Whatta you think about all that? Feeling all those extra feelings?"

Raoul shrugged, voice muffled by his knee. "Sometimes good, sometimes not-so-good."

"How's that?" Albert sat up. "Seems like a leg up over the rest of us."

The boy squinched, trying to find words. "Know how smells seep into your clothes? Some good, like incense and perfume. Some bad, like burnt peat and cigarettes. When I get close to others...it's like that, but *here*." He touched his chest. "Mamãe called it 'soaking up.' There's good things sometimes. Like your little girl. But other times..."

Suddenly the boy began to shake violently. Albert stiffened, heart in his throat, thinking the kid was lapsing into seizure. But Raoul visored his forehead, taking deep, deliberate breaths to center himself. Obviously something Lola had taught him.

"The man you shot," he said after a moment. "He shouldn't have tried to rob us. He should have explained to you. But it's soaked in. His fear, his dying. And worse: the ripples. I *feel* them. His family will suffer. His girl will get sicker. I can't get it all out of me. All this hurting. It'll happen. Like the waves. I…can't stop it."

Face sinking into hands, Raoul sobbed. Gasping convulsively. For the first time, Albert saw only a lost child.

Jesus, Remy's right.

"Kid, I—uh," Albert stammered. "I didn't…didn't know. How it all worked. That you were taking so many blows." He awkwardly patted his shoulder like a skittish visitor at a petting zoo. "Look, no more hurting people. I mean, unless we really gotta. Okay? That's a promise."

The child seemed to find some inner balance. Tears abruptly ceased. He stood up, fanning his book pages, smiling sadly: "A promise broken before it was made?"

THE BRINKGATE, of course, was in utter chaos.

Not only was Canal passage firmly shut. Not only was its narrow mouth bottlenecked with boats of desperate refugees pleading or cursing for admittance north (jammed up in such a way as to make all navigation impossible). Topping it all off, bordies had the audacity to *still be there.*

One meager squad: three men on the concrete causeway over the gate itself, four on the eastern Canal wall just ahead of Albert and Company, and two more down in the control room beyond the gate—voice droning over Brinkgate intercom. All of this evening lunacy punctuated by the steady tremolo of a world grumbling beneath their feet.

Hell ain't just other people, Albert thought, *but they don't spruce it up much.*

"You are at the Brink!" the intercom declared to the roaring crowd. "Southernmost border of the Southeast Bloc Protectorates! Only *documented* Bloc or Protectorate citizens, or those with temp visa status, are permitted beyond the gate!"

"Gotta be shittin' me." Remy laughed humorlessly. His voice filling with sudden fury. "They gonna pull this shit? *Now?* With whole world collapsin' around 'em?"

The three travelers crouched low on the wall fifty yards from the gate, taking cover behind a Canal girder.

"Just a token rearguard. Bordie protocol," Albert said. "It's politics, Remy. Border Guard brass covering their asses, making it look like they did their solemn duty."

"They's kids down there!" Remy peered down into the Canal, then roared at Albert: "Fuckin' *kids!*"

He'd never seen Remy so furious in all the years he'd known him. Albert shrank back, nodding in concession while the man fumed, chest thundering.

"Tellya what. Stay with the kid." Albert handed him the revolver. "Stay out of sight. I'll get past the bordies on the wall. Got my visa if I need it." He pointed through the mesh of the gate. "See a maintenance ladder near the control booth. I'll climb down. Get the gate open for these folks. Enough distraction for you to sneak the kid across."

"Sound like a shit plan to me. How you gonna get them open that gate?"

Albert grinned. "My wily charm."

"Oughta be *me* riskin' my ass, Allie. Ain't nothin' in the world move *you*," Remy spat.

Albert frowned, but clapped Remy's shoulder. "Yer a shit climber, Rem. This job requires finesse."

Albert vaulted the girder and the others ducked low. Remy snorted, smirking:

"Closest I get to an apology, I spose."

Albert hugged the right ledge of their three meter walkway, keeping distance from the four nearby bordermen gazing down into the crowd below. Further ahead, perpendicular on the overhanging gate archway, a bordie operated a spotlight which danced over refugee faces in the gloom like a cruel firefly. On either side of the spotlight were gun emplacements manned by antsy bordies swiveling to and fro like boys who'd seen too many war simmies.

Probably got hard-ons, dumb shits.

The path was simple enough, the wall's walkway wide and unlit, and the four bordies' backs turned. But halfway past them, Albert's heel dragged and scuffed lightly on concrete. Three of them didn't notice. The bordie at the tail end of the quartet whipped around, saw Albert, lifted his rifle.

"*Freeze!*"

"Whoa, easy." Albert laughed. "Be cool—"

"Hands! Up!" The man activated his rifle light. Albert squinted as it flared in his eyes.

"Boys, I'm a Bloc citizen returning north. Didn't wanna be a fly in yer refugee soup down there," Albert said calmly. Slowly moving his raised hands toward pockets. "I'm gonna get my visa out. I am reaching slowly for it now, so please do not—"

"Hold up a sec!" The first bordie he'd snuck past activated his own rifle light, splashed it across Albert. "Gotta be kiddin'. No…goddamn…way."

Albert recognized the voice, winced. *All the fucking luck.*

"Thought he drowned!" Pugface hooted. "This is a catch! Hooked ourselves one murderin' smuggler! It's *him*!"

"Him *who*?"

"Fucker shot Fredy!"

All four were aiming at him now.

"On the ground," Pugface ordered.

"Why?" Albert said. "So you can shoot me without a trial?"

"Wanna trial?" Pugface slammed the butt of his rifle into Albert's belly. He doubled over, vomiting. "Can't keep yer lunch down! Guilty conscience! State rests, y'Honor." The others laughed. Pugface put his boot to Albert's back, shoved him down flat. He hunted on his belt for restraints and came up empty. "Lend me yer cuffs," he said to one of his comrades.

"Hell, no. Never get 'em back. Like my lighter."

"Pook, gimme yers," he said to another. "That's a order."

"Order?" the man scoffed. "From yer dumb ass?"

The men ribbed back and forth, and all the while, ear pressed to the Canal, Albert was listening to it build. And build. A tremendous fracas amidst an already tremulous earth. He was about to say something, but someone said it for him:

"What the fuck's *that*?"

Suddenly, the boot was off his back, the bordies staring south. The spotlight craned to follow their gazes, lighting up open marshlands. Quiet fell. Albert pushed himself up to see.

Hundreds of yards out, a deep blackness was spreading over open fen. A darkness far blacker than twilight—creeping, bleeding, its way toward a section of Canal south of the Brinkgate. Albert heard the hollow slosh of bogwater rushing to fill deep cavities. And as that darkness touched the base of the Canal, concrete began to scream under the strain of rupturing earth.

He didn't waste a second, dashing north past the gate archway to reach the ladder down to gate control. *If I don't get it open for these Floridiots before the south Canal cracks…*

Someone shouted after him. Squeezing off a few lousy potshots. But they had larger concerns as the tumult of refugees below grew from unhappy murmur to howls of terror and outrage. Curses hurled. Death hexes spat. Belongings and luggage thrown heatedly, helplessly, at the sealed Brinkgate. One steamship at the rear fired up engines and careened through smaller craft to ram the gate. Someone on deck brandishing a firearm, squeezing off an errant round. The perched bordermen cowered.

"Desist!" the intercom demanded. "Desist or you will be fired upon!"

The warning was ignored as the Canal to the south began to shudder wildly.

Albert slid down the ladder twenty feet, palms burning by the time his boots slapped the landing of the control platform. He ducked against the wall beneath the booth window, retrieving the hunting knife just as a bordie exited to observe the madness through the gate mesh. His back to Albert now.

In one fluid motion, Albert seized the man about the forehead, slashed his windpipe and kneed him, gagging, into stagnant Canal water. He quickly slipped into the open control room. The second guard was turned away, yammering into the intercom:

"Final warning! Desist now or we'll be forced—" Breath sucked in.

Spotting Albert in a reflection, the guard turned to meet him, catching his knife hand as it slammed toward his exposed neck. Chamelo activated as they scuffled, the man blending with the twinkling console. Like wrestling with a ghost.

He was powerful, even pinned to the controls, staving off Albert's blade with sheer upper body strength. But his footing provided little leverage and soon his arm was quaking. Albert slammed a knee into his unplated femoral nerve and the man released an airy whimper as muscles failed. The knife tip plunging into his throat.

Albert guided the gurgling man to the floor, immediately activating the gate operation override on the panel. But the Canal shivered beneath him with distant buckling. Glancing out the view windows, he watched sluggish water move.

First coursing south. Then raging south. It wasn't the pumps.

Canal just ruptured. All this water…all these people…

He jumped out of the booth to watch the Brinkgate lift and saw scores of crowded vessels dragging back south on cataract currents. Some people leapt from ships to grapple the rising gate. Some dove for nearby jetties as their boats ripped away beneath them to fill an awful new crater.

Dozens of vessels fired up steam engines, kinetic drives, or solar cells and fought the raging water. Making for the open gate full speed ahead.

That's when the bordies opened fire.

Albert heard the *whump*ing of the mounted ETC guns above and watched as hypersonic rounds ripped through the hull of a solar cog like tissue paper. Air filled with an ozone reek as its cell-drive shorted, belching forth plumes of electrical miasma. Screaming or scorched or dismembered passengers spilling into the water like dumped cargo. Dragged south with the flow.

Albert made for the ladder, enraged. Climbing as fast as limbs would function, listening to the storm of gunfire and the tinny *rip-crunch* of another craft shredded by electrothermal-chemical strafing. Then another.

When he'd achieved the twenty foot climb, he surveyed the scene. The rest of the bordies, save the two on mounted guns over the archway, had crossed to his east Canal wall. Spread out flat on their bellies, rattling off rifle volleys into refugees below.

Big guns first. Albert dashed toward the bordie on the closest swivel gun.

He was hanging a right onto the narrow gate causeway, approaching the gun emplacement, when he heard the telltale blast of his hand cannon. Turned to see Remy advancing from cover on their wall, the body of the first prone bordie still twitching nearby. Albert watched him level the revolver at the next prostrate man in line, firing at his head and killing him instantly.

"We got kids, you sonsabitches!" Remy was screaming. *"Kids! Can't have 'em! Won't letcha have none of 'em!"*

Remy fired again but the next man's chamelo armor caught the shot. When the other two realized what was happening, all three rolled for defilade behind girders. Redirecting fire at their new threat as Remy blundered for cover.

"Remy!" Albert screamed.

The bordie at the mounted gun beside Albert flinched, saw him there, and shifted to meet him. Albert slammed a heel into the man's chest with all his weight, sending him toppling over the ledge to rushing waters below.

He grabbed the handles of the mounted gun, swiveling it to the second heavy gunner—the man aiming now for Remy's position. Squeezing the trigger, Albert watched the second emplacement erupt in sparks and slagged metal. Its operator shrieking, clawing his own scorched face as he fell.

"Goddamn butchers!" Remy screamed. *"Those're families!"*

Albert swiveled back around to cover his friend just in time to see Pugface put a round through Remy's torso. Remy stumbled backward, collapsed.

Albert was only aware that his throat was raw with screaming. He didn't recall squeezing the trigger, or the sonic *whump-whump* of his weapon's dampened recoil. But he watched the three remaining Border Guardsmen lanced against their cover like rag dolls, limbs flying apart—bone, meat and armor exploding—under his heavy flanking fire.

He stopped shooting only when the weapon overheated. The sudden silence of the world numbing. Chirps of night, gush of water, purrs of engines as several craft made it successfully through the gate.

Albert's senses returned when he heard a voice:

"Damn," Remy echoed. He crawled, hands clawing for

purchase on the nearest girder, bright trail of blood streaked behind him. "God damn. God damn, God damn…" He repeated over and over until it was unclear whether he was *God damn*ing or damning God.

Albert released the gun, ran to meet him, hurdling bodies and severed limbs. He saw Raoul rushing to meet from the opposite direction, rucksack in his little hands. Albert took the bag from him, rummaging for first aid.

"We gotcha, Rem," Albert said, kneeling. "We gotcha. Yer fine."

"God." Remy leaned back against the girder. Hacked up blood. Albert pulled open the man's flower print shirt and knew immediately antiseptics and bandages were useless. A great rent seared straight through his belly. "Damn, I feel it. I dead."

"Nope." Albert mopped at the seeping wound with bundles of gauze; tried to apply pressure. "Getting you home to yer wife and son, you moron," he panted. "Y'ain't dying."

Remy grabbed Albert's busy hands to halt him.

"Die long before I meet you." Surprisingly, hc looked up at Raoul. "*You* know it, boy. Say them words. I can't speak 'em."

Albert looked up at the kid. Raoul's flittering eyes full of tears.

"His family's dead." Hearing the words, Remy shook violently. "Displaced by that big storm. Gertie. Lost everything. Migrating inland, caught up in the Landgrabs. No work. Little food. But he wouldn't be like the others. Robbing and killing. His wife got sick, died of dysentery.

Still he wouldn't. Tried to get his son to Bloc territory. But the boy…"

Raoul couldn't go on.

"At the end, M-Manny so crazed by hunger I find him eatin' gravel…*gravel*," Remy's voice broke. "Says to m-me: 'Candy, Daddy! Candy all over the ground! The lemony kinds is best!' And he die right there in my arms. Not one m-more word."

Remy pressed fists to forehead, releasing a noise like an animal. Bereft of all human airs. Raoul knelt and hugged him. The man tensed up at human contact, but cradled the boy's head after a moment. Sobbing. Then pressed Raoul abruptly away, bloodshot eyes piercing Albert.

"Shauna, Manny…" Remy gasped, "that's closest I care to get near God. God a maniac. His game got no rules. Only getta decide who we play it for." He glanced at Raoul. "Y'gotta be a beast, be it for *them*…and no other reason." He grabbed Albert's collar. "I don't care about no heaven. Just wish they's someplace to fall before *them*. Hear they own judgment. Maybe then, ah sh-shit, mayb—"

Remy died mid-sentence.

Albert crouched awhile in silence. He attempted to close Remy's eyes but rigid eyelids wouldn't stay shut. Empty gaze indicting the world. Cursing, Albert removed his own shirt, draped it over Remy's head. When he heard the groans of a wounded bordie, he took the cannon from Remy's stiff hand and quietly stood up.

"Kid," he murmured absently, "hafta break that promise."

There was long a pause. The boy nodded.

"Anything you can do to keep from…*soaking up*?"

"I'll try." The child squeezed his eyes shut, covered ears, buried nose in his sleeve. Trying to dull his exquisite senses.

Albert approached slowly. Pugface scrabbled on the ground, helmet discarded. His right arm was a ruin, right leg severed from the shin down. Face pallid, breath ragged. Wide eyes dilated unnaturally. Albert came to a rest standing over him. The man looked up in wonder.

"Yer going into shock," Albert told him. "That's why you feel strange."

The man blinked wild eyes. "Please."

"Tell me yer name."

"D-Dan. Danny Bordt."

Albert crouched. "Got family? Loved ones? Home somewhere?"

"My mom. Up in Orlando with my sisters. P-please. Wanna go home." It became apparent for the first time how young the man was. Not a day over twenty.

"Even been laid, Danny?"

The man was sobbing now, staring at his severed leg, shaking his head spastically. "Want my mom," he sputtered. "*M-Mom.*"

Albert nodded. "Easy to kill nameless men. Like squashing bugs." He grabbed him by the carapace, pulled him close. "Ain't a real killer, Danny, 'less you know what yer killing."

Jamming the pistol under his jaw, he watched the man's scalp erupt. A mist of brain and bone fragment. Eyes rolling with the same vacant awe he'd seen in faces of freebooters years ago. Those he'd hunted down.

Albert let the man slump. He dropped his pistol, sat

down amidst dead bordies pretzel-style. A man at a grue-some picnic. Peering into moon-glazed Canal water, he considered the sniveling thug. And his own mother, raped and murdered by such man-children. And Remy. Not the smart-ass captain, but a shattered husband and father resurfacing at death. Someone he'd never known.

Out of sight of the boy, beneath a clear starry sky, Albert wept silently for all things ground down, laid waste —never to be whole again.

PART 3

AFTERSHOCKS

FATHER AND SON quit the Canal for good.

At first, proceeding north along the ramparts, they'd hoped for a stray ship. But channel currents had been too terrible for anything to linger long, and the earth beneath the Canal had grown increasingly restless.

A day out, Albert and Raoul had turned to watch a large section of channel south of the Brinkgate fully collapse into a sinkhole, setting off chain reactions of subsidence for much of the day. Not as dramatic as the fall of Okeechobee, but symptomatic of rampant erosion beneath the Canal itself. A pitfall waiting to give.

When they discovered a maintenance ladder leading down to the marsh floor, Albert made the tough choice to abandon their high road, head northeast across swampland for the trade town of Kissimmee. He supposed they were far enough inland to elude tsunamis and, anyway, they'd never hike the full 300 miles of Canal to Capital Landing. From Kissimmee, they could push just north to the city of Orlando. Only real oasis of civilization in Central Florida…and last chance of evac home to Tallahassee.

Just keep eyes peeled for beasts.

They trudged for hours across bogs largely drained to southern sinkholes. Terrain unflooded but pitted, muddy and difficult to negotiate. Twice Raoul lost a shoe, the two of them shoveling up mounds of gunk to retrieve it. The boy was looking squalid. Caked in grime, tanned skin blanched and clammy. At first, Albert thought he was only melancholy and miserable, but his breathing sounded labored.

"What's amatter?"

"Nothing," Raoul said. "Just thirsty."

Albert stopped. "Why didn't you say so? We got clean water."

"Didn't want to bother you."

"Damn it all. If yer thirsty, bother me."

"Okay, Mr. Fountain."

Albert took a water bottle from his rucksack, handed it to the boy. Watched him take several long pulls. When he handed it back, Albert took a drink himself before stowing the bottle. Glancing at the torpid child. "Y'alright? Sleepy?"

"It's okay." Raoul started to walk. "My legs are just a little wobbly."

"Soon as we find a dry patch, we'll take a rest."

Raoul nodded.

Albert didn't like his demeanor. The kid was usually sharp as a tack. He held the back of his hand to Raoul's forehead. *Headed for heatstroke.*

"C'mere…" Albert unslung the sacks from his back, stowed the boy's book, tucking it all under an arm. Then knelt to the ground, inviting the child to wrap arms around his collar. He stood up with Raoul on his back, bounced him once to make sure grips were secure, then plodded on across the empty fen. "When I was a kid, we called this a piggyback ride."

"*Piggyback*," Raoul tried out the word, giggled quietly. "Why?"

"Uh, well…" He paused theatrically. "See, before men, *pigs* ruled the earth. Their stumpy little legs were no good for riding horseback, so humans served as their horses. A pig lord would cry out…" Albert attempted an English burr: " 'You there, human boy! I require transport to town!' And if you were that boy, you'd hafta obey. Give yer pig lord a lift."

The boy laughed aloud. "That's not true at all."

"The truth is boring."

"Why'd you really call it a piggyback?"

Albert shrugged beneath weight of boy and sacks. "Just supposed to be fun or something." He peeked back. "Is it?"

"Pretty much."

"Mission accomplished."

They quietly lumbered on, listening to mud squelch under Albert's boots. Scanning abutting plains drab beneath an overcast sky. Albert recognized the snaking curve of an old state road or highway up ahead, but it was largely lost in coagulated films of muck.

An ancient billboard structure rose above it. Whatever it once advertised shredded, faded by the ages. But an embossed plastic effigy remained prominent: features sun-bleached, but looking like some sort of cartoon animal. Big round ears—a bear, a mouse? Albert pointed silently and the boy grunted in amusement. But he was still hung up on pigs:

"All the pigs in the world…" Raoul said, "they're gone?"

"Dunno. All the pigs in the *Bloc* are gone. Nutricides did most in," he said. "But they still refab pork. Their genome's stocked in most genebanks."

"If they can refabricate their meat, why can't they refabricate a pig?"

Albert shrugged. "Could if they want. Hardly anyone wanted 'em as pets when they were around. Pigs were bred as livestock. For slaughterhouses." He grunted. "Guess they figure it's pretty mean. Bring an extinct thing back to life… just to kill it for food."

Or less profitable, he kept to himself.

They were silent for many moments as they walked.

"A pet pig would be so cool," Raoul finally said.

"Yeah?" Albert nodded. "*Would* be pretty damn sweet."

RAOUL MAY HAVE NEEDED little sleep but Albert was staggering, bone-tired. When it began drizzling around late afternoon, they took shelter in an old tumbledown barn amidst a clearing. Ground floor was a mud sink, so they climbed up into the second-story loft to repose. Albert doled out food and drink from their stock, but conked out before even eating.

Sleep didn't last long. Grisly nightmares of unremitting violence brought him screaming awake. From a dark corner of the loft, Raoul watched him.

"How long's it been?" Albert steadied his trembling voice as he sat up.

"Couple hours. I think."

Albert nodded. Rising, he peered out the loft window. Night had come and the stars were out. The marshlands quiet and windless over the spasmodic rumbling of the earth.

"You didn't kill him," Raoul said.

"What? Who?"

"Remy. In your dream you killed him. Put a gun under his chin."

Albert frowned. "Thought you can't read minds."

"You talk in your sleep." The boy took out his book.

Albert shivered in the muggy heat, but nodded, approaching the boy. "Said you see stories in the pictures sometimes. That book of yers. Whattaya see in there?"

"Lots of things." The boy turned the book in his hands. "Big cities by big lakes. Or scary camps in cold mountains. Or big desert battles. Strange places and people. Depends on how I look at the pictures. Some-times…" he paused, "…I think I see *us* on the pages."

"Gotta few words for whatever asshole wrote *that* story," Albert snorted, taking the book a moment. Squinting at a random page: a cave painting-esque diagram of…a woman holding hands with a crystal giant? He shrugged and handed it back, glancing at the child's untouched rations. "You never ate."

"I'm not hungry."

"Need to eat."

"I can't," the child moaned suddenly. "My stomach."

Moving closer to study him, Albert realized the boy had been sick; had retched over the ledge into the mud below. His whole body trembling. Albert knelt before him and felt his head. *Jesus, ain't heatstroke. He's on fire.*

"How you feel?"

The boy clutched his own shoulders. "I'm cold."

"How long you been puking?"

"All night."

"Goddamnit!" he barked. "How come you didn't say nothing?"

The boy hugged his book. "Remy made you feel bad. Scolded you. But you don't want me, Mr. Fountain. I was Mãe's choice, not yours. You don't know what to do with me, even if we make it out of here. And now that I'm sick…" He left the rest unsaid, only shrugging.

Albert's jaw flexed. "We're leaving together, kid."

"You're ashamed about how you really feel."

"Don't care how I really feel." Saying it made it true. "Men like me…our feelings…you can't trust those. I only trust what I'm capable of. I'm getting you outta here. Needja to believe that."

For the first time, Albert saw pure surprise in the boy's face.

"Drink. It flushes out sickness. And try to make yourself sleep. Helps the body get better. We'll leave at first light. Getcha medicine at the trade town."

"Okay."

Albert placed two water bottles within the boy's reach, then upended their two rucksacks, bundling the empty canvasses over Raoul in lieu of a blanket. He paced back to the loft opening and looked out at starry swamplands, too restless for sleep.

"You didn't kill him, Mr. Fountain," the boy whispered drowsily.

"Didn't save him neither," Albert murmured. "Yer the only one ever really tried."

REST AND FLUID did Raoul little good. By mid-morning the next day, as Albert led them northeast across a sludgy mire, the boy was dazed and pale and retching intermittently. Seeing Raoul was in no condition for travel, Albert took the book out of the boy's hands, stored it in their sacks.

"I need it," the boy insisted.

"No, you don't."

"Need to look *again*," Raoul spluttered deliriously. "I think—I saw—"

"It's safer in the bag. I promise." He picked up the boy, flesh hot to the touch. "Remember anything biting you?"

"I dunno."

"Any bugs or anything?"

"Dunno."

After another sleepless night, Albert was utterly spent. But he walked faster, feet kicking up small geysers of gunk. They'd probably reach the outskirts by afternoon. But this was no head cold. If the boy had caught something, time was not on their side.

They followed brushwood along a forest edge, approaching a narrow glade on their left carved ages ago for the collapsed tower of a power line array. Just as they cleared the scrubby tree line, Albert stopped dead in his tracks.

Ten yards down the glade. A splashing, corkscrewing pounce of motion. Jerking, lethal. He didn't know what the gatorbrid was killing, but the doomed creature thrashed in its clutches. He watched the reptile twirl, ridged spine looping serpent-like as it drowned its prey in pools of muck.

Albert wanted his gun. Holding Raoul, he couldn't chance the motion.

No one knew who'd revived them from extinction, but the culprit hadn't left their genome unmodded. One of many splice-job vanity projects by would-be "genic artists" hungry for notoriety in a discipline long-dominated by Brasilia. The original species was already a fast, deadly hunter. But a rigid vertebrae made it clumsy at land-based course correction. Its protracted snout could snap bone, but was slow to reopen, easily bound shut.

The resurrected variant was spliced with a coiling spinal column for lightning-quick turns; bulky, abridged snout for rapid snapping. Pronounced, muscular limbs for land stalking with opposable paws for subduing prey. A nightmare of genetic engineering…and staring now.

Eyes glinted—two gilded slits of saurian malice.

The gatorbrid abandoned its meager prey, twisting its scaled mass to face Albert and Raoul. Heartier fare. A front paw lifted delicately from the mud and hovered a moment: either test or challenge.

Albert immediately fled. Clutching the child to his chest, pumping legs as hard as he could, he sprinted east along the tree line. Mind aflood with the time-elastic high of adrenaline. The fury of his flight making it difficult to listen for the gatorbrid's pursuit.

After a spell, he ducked into the woods, recalling that gatorbrids—skilled at hunting open swamp—had difficulty negotiating thick woodland floor. He sat the boy on a knee while he unholstered his revolver. Listening, waiting. Realizing Raoul had spoken.

"What?" Albert whispered.

"It smells us," the boy murmured. "It's *coming*."

Albert flinched at a nearby splash. Scanned the direction it had come from. Only ripples settling in turbid pools. Not deep enough for it to be hiding beneath the surface. Albert felt dazed, but gripped the boy tighter, rising on squatted legs to see farther. His vantage was clear. Only trees and still water. But he heard a guttural purring from somewhere ahead. Deep and alien. Just as he was ready to slip deeper into the woods, two things happened at once.

First, he fully remembered what he'd heard of their hunting patterns:

Fast in open swamp, clumsy on forest ground…

Second, a tree bough above them bulged with girth…

But excellent climbers.

A translucent lid up there winked over a golden eye.

Albert leapt back, toppling, just as the mammoth reptile pounced. Missing them by a foot, mud erupting in filthy showers. Albert lost his pistol, pulling back legs just as the gatorbrid's jaws shut on open air. A snap of jowls like marble slabs clapped together; impact vibrating in their spines.

Flat on his back now, Albert kicked as hard as he could, praying his feet weren't caught in an open maw. He felt heels connect with a tremendous thud. Heard the creature writhe and hiss, stupefied by the blow to its snout.

He turned to hunt for his fallen gun, but his whole body wrenched backward with appalling force. The creature had chomped down on his rucksacks, yanking him off his feet. Spooky articulation of prehensile paws grabbing at him for a killing purchase.

Screaming, Albert wriggled out of the rucksack straps, hoisting the boy and sprinting deeper into the woods. Ducking branches, hurdling roots. This time he heard the gatorbrid loud and clear: a nightmarish scrabbling of appendages upon earthen floor as the blood-crazed beast scurried after them. Barking and bellowing its anthem of primordial appetites. *He's slower in here. But so am I.*

Albert nearly lost footing twice, but spotted daylight ahead and burned his last energy reserve for a boost of speed. Spilling out into the small clearing, he saw the old shed, immediately pushing the boy up to a low roof ledge.

"Climb!" he screamed. Raoul didn't need to be told twice.

As Albert scrambled to scale the shack, Raoul pulling

at his forearms to help him, they heard the gatorbrid clamber out of the tree line. Pattering across open ground now at full speed. Closing. Albert felt a muscle in his forearm herniate—yelping with the strain—but pulled until he had enough leverage to roll his body up onto the gradient.

They went still. All was silent. Then Raoul threw up.

Fitting response.

Albert's head swam with fatigue, spots dancing in his vision. Losing consciousness, but forcing himself to stand. It was doubtful the gatorbrid could jump this high from ground level, but he'd underestimated it once already. Glancing carefully over the ledge, he'd walked the whole perimeter before finally spotting it.

It hadn't given up. At the tiny shed's base, the reptile was quietly circling, looking for a lower wall or handhold to climb.

"Tough luck, you sonuvabitch," he wheezed. "Go eat a glasshead or something."

As if in response, the gatorbrid pounced at the wall, slamming into corrugated sheet metal and flopping back in the mud. The whole shed quaked.

Albert fell back onto his ass, laughing at the creature. Laughing at himself. It soon took on a lunatic aspect. Pure, hopeless mania. His head spinning again.

Less than half an hour. That's how long it took to lose your direction, food, first aid, your weapon, Raoul's only keepsake from his mother…and now our lives. Just can't keep a promise.

Passing out in earnest, the world around him grew fluid. Impressionist tropic smears. He observed sight and sound like a child half-listening to a bedtime story.

In that storybook, a voice cried: *"Lights! Look!"* He wasn't sure if it was a child, or himself. Thunder clapped terrifically and their tormenting Beast was vanquished. Its wicked brain bursting from a demon skull. *Deus ex machina*, Albert thought, snorting. A phrase his mother had taught him. He watched ranks of angels arrive with scepters of light, weaving from the forests to the rescue. And chuckled to himself.

Ain't it what we're all waiting for, Ma? God to descend for a cheap resolution?

At last, his world a hurricane blur, blackness swallowed Albert completely.

HE HAD NO DREAMS. There was timeless blackness followed by buttery afternoon light. Albert's eyes fluttered open, studying a vaulted ceiling with hand-hewn beams of varnished wood. He turned to the room's only light source: an ornate bay window. Blinking out at broad, leafy oaks lining a belltower of ancient, white-washed masonry. The sun-kissed estate decorated with clay amphora jars of lush Christmas cactus, runty weeping figs.

Still asleep, he thought.

Turning from the window, Albert inspected the bedroom. Cream-colored walls and hardwood floors, both adorned with intricate rugs of old Spanish design. And beneath him, a king-sized bed of softest latex foam. He was bouncing on its plushness when he noticed the woman watching from the arched doorway.

Albert sat up, startled. He couldn't find words right

away, so he studied her. Young and pretty in her flower-printed sundress. Bare feet on hardwood looking less slovenly than simply unfettered. Something about her reminded him of his wife. Except Audrey's hair was red; the woman's locks were chestnut brown.

"Am I dead?" Albert said.

The woman shook her head.

"Dreaming, then?"

"All of life is a dream." Her voice airy and sweet. Pupils, he noticed, large as saucers.

"What is this place?"

The woman scratched her calf muscle with a bare toe, but said nothing.

"You the one who saved us back there? In the woods?"

She smiled broadly now, but still said nothing.

Chick's a bit touched. Albert blew air through his lips as he climbed from the bed and realized he was naked. He covered up with a pillow, seeing his fresh-washed clothes on a wooden dresser top. Nodding at the girl in appreciation, he shyly dressed himself.

"There someone here I can talk to?" he said slowly, as if addressing a child.

The woman's face lit up now, nodding fervently as she offered a dainty hand.

"He's been waiting for you to ask after him."

It was a beautiful old Spanish-style ranch house. White-washed brick and Spanish roof tile. Rustic belltower, turrets, balconies of heavy timber splashed in aquamarines evoking a lost Mediterranean.

Elsa, the woman, insisted on holding hands during the brief tour. It seemed passing strange to Albert, but after days of dirt and sweat and gore, he couldn't argue with holding a pretty girl's hand. She led him through an empty library, across vaulted interiors furbished with carved antiques of old Europe, down an intricate circular staircase, and, *finally*, out onto a large interior courtyard tiled in smooth majolica. Central fountain trickling from cherub statuary.

A group of people played a sort of game at the farthest end. Some crouched in a circle, others on the side lines looking on. Young adults of all ages—strapping men, spry women, lanky teenagers.

Spectating from Albert's side was a man seated on a wicker lounge chair. He was slight and fat. Not obesely so, but more plump than most Americans Albert had encountered outside of pics and holos from pre-nutricide times. Wearing a roomy blue fishing shirt, cargo shorts, and flip-flops. A cheerful, ruddy complexion beneath a salt-and-pepper beard—all shaded under the brim of an old panama hat. Fingers wrapped around a glass of iced tea, lips locked in a grin. Watching young people play with eyes so dark they looked like beads of obsidian glass.

"Sit yourself on down. Take a load off," he said without looking up. Voice a pleasant tenor. "Thankie much, Elsa dear."

The woman nodded at the man, moving excitedly to join her peers. Albert sat down slowly on the twin wicker chair. A second glass of iced tea perspired on a table between them. He glanced at it, throat parched.

The man watched the game raptly for several moments longer. One girl pacing the seated circle, tapping heads. Chanting, "Duck…duck…duck…." When she finally cried, *"goose!"* the chosen young man rose, chased her around the circle. Both giggling breathlessly.

Albert's host chuckled in high spirits; at last, gesturing to the drink. "Well, quench your thirst, my man."

Albert grabbed the glass, gulping down a quarter of the sweetened drink. Paused for a breath, then took another swill before wiping his mouth and addressing the man:

"Who are you?"

"Mama named me Solomon. No, I'm not of the Hebrew persuasion." The man looked at him with jet-black eyes, smiled. "She was a Floridian river slut made pregnant by a john."

Pausing for a sip of tea, the plump man sighed and smacked his lips.

"Wretched mother," he continued. "But I felt for her. Beguiled by the Rift, by men's appetites, and soon beguiled by fairy tales from Soto's missionaries." He grunted. "Not the conquistador, mind you. I'm not that old! I'm talking Padre Teo, Slayer of Sonora, the *Holy Cartel Lord*, paving way for his Virgin Army's blitz. Funny how history repeats." He laughed. "Mama loved their Judgment of King Solomon, whom so deftly gleaned a mother's love."

Albert blinked. "You've…lost me."

"Haven't heard that one? Funniest Old Testament joke, besides sad Job." He leaned forward. "Two women claim a child as their own. Bring it before the King for judgment. What Solomon suggests is: slice the babe in two, one half for each. See which woman protests. Thus divining who sees more than inherited property. Who wields a mother's love."

"I mean, I don't get *this*." Albert nodded to the ranch around them. "Where are we? Who are you?"

"*This*," the man spread his hands in an all-encompassing motion, "we call the Casa. A refuge of privacy and primacy. And *I*," he touched his chest, "have already given you my name. Solomon Carr. Call me Sol. Or Uncle. Or Uncle Sol."

Albert sat up. "Yer *the* Uncle? Like, the *Uncle* uncle?"

"If it please you."

"It's a local myth," Albert scoffed.

"Mythology's a rousing perfume," said the Uncle, "covering odors of established realities. Helps keep brigands and thieves away. Lovely stuff, really."

Albert chewed his lip a moment, sizing the man up. "You a real uncle?"

Solomon shrugged. "To the ancients, an uncle's duty was accepting the legacy of a dead heir. His household, his wives, children, debts. Uncles were mere *catch basins* collecting the obligations of failed lords." He grinned broadly, almost proudly. "Such is the plight of lesser sons."

"Lotta folks over there." Albert glanced at the giggling, multiethnic crowd. "Which are yers?"

"*All.*"

"Big family."

"The biggest." The Uncle did not blink. "An uncle to all Man."

"Ah." Albert sat back, sighed. "I get it. Yer an evangelist or something."

"Goodness, no. You'll find no mysticism here. No angels or demons. Promises of heavenly reward for earthly service rendered. *God*," he spat the word. "God is a parent *fucking*—excuse my French—without thought for what's begotten. But an *uncle*—ah! He's a child amongst children. Nothing is his by design. Love is his choice, never his need. If anyone best understands love, it is uncle." He tasted his words, nodded. "It belongs to no God. Gods, like fathers, rarely earn it. Only demand it."

Albert's head was reeling. "So, what *are* you exactly?"

Solomon seemed bemused. "Said it yourself: a *family*. No pedigree. No blood relation. United by accident, choosing each other. The purest family."

Last halfway house at the world's end. These patron-types. Saving the earth one orphan at a time. "Where's the boy?"

"Your boy?" the Uncle clarified. "Being seen to. Poor soul was in first stages of vivax malaria. Rampant in some parts, I'm afraid. We've no nanomeds out here, but he's reacting astonishingly well to old world treatment. Strong boy. Incredible immune system. We'll check on him soon."

"Sound like a learned man," Albert observed. "You a doctor?"

He shook his head. "Just an avid reader."

"Didn't see any devices or books inside. Just an empty library," Albert laughed genially. "And, no offense, but you don't look the sort to get Haze-rigged."

"I burn every book after reading."

Albert laughed until he saw it wasn't a joke. "My, uh,

boy lost a favorite of his. The Swallowed World. Don't suppose you'd have a copy on hand?"

"An idea set in ink seeks immortality on flaking paper. If you ask me, something not absorbed on first reading," he tapped his temple, "is not worth absorbing."

Albert slouched into his chair, shook his head. *What a riot.* "Anyway, I'm Albert. And thank you for this. We were…" Albert chuckled bleakly, "…certainly in a jam. Anything I can do to repay you?"

"Gratitude's more priceless than gifts, I think. But mayhaps I can trouble you for a walk?" The Uncle's eyes looked forlorn, voice lowering confidentially: "Not often I get to shoot the shit with men closer my age."

Albert threw hands up. "Of course."

"Peachy!" He turned to the young people. "My dears, we're all going for a walk!"

Spinning at Sol's call, they abandoned their game with a giggling chorus of *yes-Uncle*s.

A WELL-MAINTAINED PATH ran the perimeter of the massive ranch house, shaded by canopies of old oaks as the sun dipped west. Albert and Sol moseyed side by side, the rest of the group several paces back. He smelled barbecue in the open air and salivated.

Would it be rude to wring a dinner outta my host?

Albert strolled with one hand in pocket, the other holding his drained glass. Admiring the ranch's brick work, scaly Spanish roof tiles, painted timber verandas.

"Place's beautiful," he marveled. "How you maintain it without Bloc stipend?"

The Uncle adjusted the hat on his head and smiled through his grizzly beard. "Every family member has his or her household duty, and no duty is shirked. Price of family."

Albert glanced back at the following group. Some of them leaping to catch moths. A giggle here or there. "Yer not worried about all the ruckus?" Albert said. "The tsunamis, the cave-ins?"

"No use getting bent out of shape over a couple aftershocks."

"Oughta think about getting north. Like me and Raoul."

"This is our *home*." The man's black eyes looked appalled at the suggestion.

Albert nodded silently and let it lie, seeing he'd touched a nerve. They passed a pair of ancient automobiles retrofitted with solar cells. Pickups with massive all-terrain tires, great cages in their truck beds. Albert glanced at them casually, wondering if he could somehow finagle one.

"Y'know," he scoffed, "I hear a lotta goofy-ass stories about you."

"Oh?" the Uncle perked up. "Let's have one."

"Just idiot superstition." He glanced at the trucks again. "You certainly don't ride around straddling a gatorbrid."

The Uncle laughed in incredulity. "One tired old cliché rings true: folks do fear what they don't comprehend."

"They do." Thinking of his initial reaction to Raoul, Albert had to agree. "Yes, we do." He looked at Uncle Sol. "So, what's it you all do out here?"

"Duties no one else shoulders. Toil on the land in the olden, golden ways." His eyes shone with pride.

Liable to drown down here with your olden, golden ways. "Farming and stuff, huh?"

Uncle Sol nodded. "We harvest a rare crop."

Dope? Albert thought. *Can't be too lucrative from one ranch. South America's got these clowns beat a million times over.*

The Uncle squinted up at Albert. "Care for a quick peek?"

Albert shrugged. He really wanted to get Raoul and be on their way. But the thought of a hearty meal at this rainbow's end was tempting. He said: "Uh, sure."

He'd remember this moment later and rue that he'd not fled at once.

AT FIRST, entering the Casa's vast farm yards south of the ranch, Albert thought he was hearing noises of sheep or other livestock—refabbed or untouched by the nutricides. It wasn't. In the last mauve light of day, as their group paraded down to a clearing where an ancient plantation had once stood, Albert saw...*people.*

All colors, all creeds. People locked moaning in sheds; people caged in wood-rotted husks of animal pens; people bound to maypoles by necks or wrists, shambling in exhausted circles like thrall dancers of some dread festival.

Albert froze in his tracks. The group of young people behind him swarmed very close. Almost touching, body heat emanating.

Words failed him.

The Uncle proceeded forward to stand at the center of the grassy grounds. Between a raging bonfire and a wide pitfall lidded with enmeshed tree branches. He raised hands almost in benediction.

Albert stopped breathing. Listening to strains of human misery. His voice surprisingly tempered: "What…is this?"

"The harvest grounds," Uncle said.

More of the Uncle's brood were overseeing prisoners with machetes or old kalashnikov rifles. The eyes of captives sunken and feral. Some whimpered or openly wept, but many simply gazed out from haunted faces— faces beyond all despair. Forty or fifty in all.

Albert glanced at the pitfall, sensing animal movement; glanced at the bonfire, smelling cooked meat again. Not wanting to know what was barbecuing. His head swam.

"Here's where you'll stay for the duration."

Albert could only blink. "Of?"

"Your time on this earth."

Many hands rested on him now. His shoulders, arms, back. Not firmly—with the limpness of possessors convinced of their ownership. Albert didn't resist them. Something in their manner told him it would spell swift death.

"Nurse a man back to health just to kill him?"

"*Kill* you?" the Uncle laughed. "Beside the point. A father must feel the slide. The breakdown from sage creature to sheer chemical basis. Elsewise, he's a weak harvest, isn't he? Pure chaff."

Anger boiled up. "*Harvest?*"

Uncle Sol smiled, turned to address someone behind

Albert: "Elsa, dear, we've fresh crop to till. Won't you show Albert how it's done?"

The pretty woman in the sundress pushed forward past Albert.

"Yes, Uncle," she said, surveying the squalid captives. "I see lots who are ready."

"The ripest, darling, the *ripest*. Uncle's watching."

Albert glanced back at the others. Their eyes dilated to naught but pupils, enraptured by Elsa.

The dainty woman plucked a bayonet from a wooden table, studied the blade a moment. Then moved to a man tied to a maypole. A neo-Seminole in befouled patchwork regalia. The man chanted to himself with eyes closed until Elsa, with one playful swipe, opened his trachea. He could only mewl thinly as she set about stabbing him. Over and over—out and plunge—until her hand was a blur of blood and steel; his body dangling from bound wrists.

"Excellent choice, Elsa!" the Uncle clapped. "All those neos. Neo-Confucians, neo-Fascists, the neo-Marxists and neo-pagans! All who reach for dead pasts! Ripe! Ripe!"

Elsa moved immediately to someone else. When the blonde woman saw Elsa coming, she began crying and screeched: "Mother...*mother*!" Elsa speared her throat to shut her up. Then, calmly withdrawing, pierced and pierced her stomach until rope creaked with dead weight. Albert's blood froze solid when he recognized the delicate bulge of the slain young woman's pregnant belly. The gravity of her plea sinking in.

"That one wasn't so ripe, dear. Cried mummy."

"They're *people*, goddamnit!" Albert shouted.

"Man is a beast divorced from nature. A chimera."

Solomon turned back to Albert. "Intellect seals that annulment. Our *awareness* separates us. Right, my dears?"

The Uncle's brood answered with a chorus of *yes-Uncle*s.

The Uncle walked to the weapon table, retrieved a machete. "Oh, it's freakish—awareness. More resilient than our animal meat, but it tortures this meat dearly. Nature has no such issue. Rots from within with no thought or care." He chopped the dead Native American down from the maypole. Dragged him with curious strength toward the bonfire. "But Humankind," he continued, "is a creature of *mind*. More durable stuff. Transcends the flesh. Man knows Nature's breast offers only mindless death, but still He sips. He hates it—being alone with His awful *knowing*. It's why He lies. Why He wars. Why He orphans His babes. *Cowardice*."

Solomon began hacking the man to pieces, limb by limb, doling out sinewy parts between the pit and the roaring fire. The fire crackling with roasted blood.

"Uncle, folks is such cowards!" someone cried.

"I know, Wendy. Uncle knows." The Uncle halted butchering and clucked his tongue. "Mankind could be gorgeous. Make all things new. Instead, He swallows death and makes it true. So, I oblige Him." He tossed a severed calf into the pit. Albert heard the bellow of a familiar reptile. "If He'd rather forego all that He is, all He sires, Uncle will intercede. Uncle will tuck everyone in. Till the last man's perished with his Earth."

Panting, he finished distributing the butchered man. His brood howling in ecstasy. Several of them moved out to the harvest grounds and went to work. Albert had to clench his eyes shut at the frenzied commotion of murder.

"Why?" he gasped.

"Why *what*?" the Uncle laughed.

"Why are you doing this?"

"Ask why a star blazes." He lifted gore-slathered hands to the night above. "I act in accordance with my makeup. My most honest reaction to life is hate."

Albert was almost hyperventilating. "Don't know me. How can you hate me?"

"Don't hate one man. I hate *all* men," Uncle said. "And women. And all new gradations betwixt and between. No difference! All hold power to improvise the ancient dances. Instead they covet them, ape them. Lo! They detest the very human faculty!"

The brood cheered.

Albert threw Uncle's own words back at him: "But you understand *love* best."

"And how!" The Uncle was delighted by the riposte. "It's a first step toward hate. True love is understanding. True hate? A verdict on that understanding. I hate Man most, for of all living things I *love* Man most. Back and forth he frolics! Mind to flesh, mind to flesh. A lovely, hateful dance which must be addressed." He slapped bloody hands on his thighs. "I'm not complicated. No riddles, no motives encrypted in lyrics. I love, I hate, and participate."

Albert tried to lunge at him, but his head was woozy. Something in the tea. Many hands pulled him gently back.

"Yes! Good! I am not exempt!" Solomon Carr pirouetted in the firelight. "But I hate myself least."

"Better than the rest of us?" Albert hissed.

"Oh no, my dear. *Worse*." The Uncle approached, hefting the machete. Grinning. "The worst man I know of. It's what qualifies me for the task. My dance is most ancient. No denial. No creeds. No excuses for my conduct." His face was close enough to kiss. "I wish to maim, you see. To ruin. To do irreparable harm. I wish to burn everyone right down to their common element, dance in the light of their burning. If I've one secret wish, it's to be *surprised*." He laughed off such nonsense. "But I'm perfectly content to be that last man who leaves…putting out every last light."

Albert was seeing things now. Shapes flickered in an out of existence. Fires spiraling like confetti serpents.

The Uncle's face swelled like a parade float balloon. Eyes two black singularities from which no light could escape.

"Shall we show him?" the Uncle cried. "That we are not biased?"

Everyone cheered, hooted, laughed.

"Philip, my boy."

"Yes, Uncle." A muscly teen stepped forward. The one who'd chased the girl in the game—the *goose*.

"My love, won't you help me make the truth burn brighter?"

Philip took a breath, knelt before his shorter master. "Love you, Uncle."

The Uncle smirked and touched the young man's cheek. Then strangled him. Philip's eyes bulged without complaint. Someone behind Albert said: "Goodbye, Philip." And then another, and another. A cheerful chorus of *Goodbye-Philip*s and *Love-you-Philip*s while the Uncle throttled and throttled his brawny, young disciple. Philip slobbered and gurgled, finally slumping into the older man's arms.

Kissing the young man's sweat-beaded brow, the Uncle dragged him to the fire, one woman helping him heave the whole body onto the blaze. Sharing nothing with the beasts in the pit.

Albert retched now. As the Uncle returned, he broke loose and attacked him. His senses were gloopy, but he dragged the man to the ground. Pounded him with rubbery fists. The Uncle hooted like a man roughhousing with a pup until his brood pulled Albert gently away.

"Where is the boy?" Albert shouted.

"Most become men," the Uncle teased.

"My *son*!"

The brood hauled him to the maypole.

"Like all fathers, you squirted him out. Recoiled. Regretted. And now, at last, relinquished him." Solomon dusted grass from his shorts, watched them fasten Albert's wrists with fresh lengths of binding. "I see that knowing ripen! It diminishes you. And when you've broken down to your *honest* elements…"

Albert writhed and screamed but the Uncle's merry tenor drowned out all noise:

"…you'll be fit to harvest."

I want my son, he thought absently.

Days had no beginning, nights no end. They kept him

doped up. Called it "Uncle's Brew." Iced tea infused with some narcotic. At first Albert had refused it, but it was all they offered for drink and, eventually, he guzzled each serving greedily. The world swam—a flowing, molten, fickle thing. His mind twisted in stomach-turning vertigo, terrified at how unreliable reality had become...

Once he saw his wife Audrey help Elsa butcher a husband and wife, both bleating like lambs. Once he saw his own father crawl up from the gatorbrid pit, cackling like his old freebooter captors, and ordered Albert to take off his fucking clothes. At one point, he spied Lola lounging naked in the bonfire flames, laughing and pointing at her own pregnant paunch. Upon that belly dome, Albert's miniature mother was spreading her legs eagerly for slavering rapists.

Albert recoiled from the visions, clinging to his mantra.

I want my son.

The Uncle visited him often, his voice almost comforting: "There are several hallucinogens native to Florida. Passion flower, belladonna, heliotrope, morning glory..." he sang. "Processed properly, they peel back all of life's lovely lies."

"I want my son."

The Uncle smiled as he walked away. "You've no son."

After moments of silence, Albert heard a snort from somewhere nearby.

"Dunno what you did to make him work on you the way he is," a high, ragged voice said, "but don't rub it off on me."

Albert turned to see a wraith of a woman bound by the neck, hunkered down in the mud, grappling their central maypole for support. So wasted and begrimed he could tell neither age nor ethnicity.

"What's yer name?" he said.

"What's it matter?"

"How long—" He had to clear his raw throat. "How long you been here?"

Glassy dark eyes lolled in their sockets, her shrug so slight it almost never happened. "Figure I always been."

Albert watched her expectantly, but she only turned toward the mud, forgetting him.

Time seemed to ooze backward and forward. He watched the ranch house collapse into boiling waters only to resurface like a holo on rewind. He watched men and women reduced to empty-gazed livestock, butchered more as a matter of procedure than cruelty, and fed to pit or fire. Everything they ever were rose in great plumes of greasy smoke and somehow he *knew* them all. That one was Julia and that one Frank. That one Werner and that one Irene. Knowledge terrifying less for its uncanniness than its revelations of what was burning…

Here a mother with a voice like a nightingale; there a son with a talent for architecture; here a lover who only has eyes for his Helga; there a widow who finds solace in gardening. So much meaning reduced to ash.

Just as the Uncle promised.

"I want my son."

"We relinquish all progeny."

The nameless woman was right: the Uncle was paying him more attention than any other captive. Dark eyes gleaming with some cold and blank compulsion, feeding him cups of Brew from his own hand. Albert couldn't imagine why until the man confessed, whispering eagerly:

"When I saw you, I knew what you were. A gift from the Void for all my tireless efforts." He petted Albert's head like a mangy dog. "A specter of mine own father."

Albert pulled away, disgusted, and the Uncle laughed. But as the man left, the world grew unstable again. Endless songs of agony. Processions of vacant-eyed humans reduced to cinders, to fodder. The blaze never dwindled, the gatorbrids never went hungry; fresh captives arriving by truckloads to meet the same fate. The world's *only* fate: eternal collapse. On and on till the dissolution of all structure, all harmony.

"Make it worse by takin' it personal," the nameless woman murmured through cracked lips.

Albert looked at that gaunt creature by the pole. "What's it to you?"

She shook her head, murmured under her breath:

"Think yer dealin' with folks. Folks playact at goodness, playact evil." Her gaze passed from Albert as if he were a figment, scanning the impartial carnage around them. "But there's no playactin' behind *their* eyes. No care and no meanness, even."

He considered those lucid words. "Tell me yer name."

She only snorted and slumped back exhaustedly onto her bony haunches, clasping the maypole. But Albert spotted a dull glint of tarnished gold on her left ring finger.

"Didn't come here alone, did you?"

She squinted at him awhile, so long Albert figured she hadn't heard the question. But all of a sudden she was rambling tonelessly: "They raided our homestead, hauled

127

us all here in cages. Killed my granddaughter first. She was, I think…fifteen? *Fourteen*. They hold onto some kids that age, but not her. She kept lookin' at her daddy, but he could do nothin' but shout himself raw.

"They chose him next; suppose they saw him flicker out inside. That was his baby girl. Hardly made a sound when they set upon him with bolos." Her fingers were drumming a wild staccato rhythm on the pole. "Tried to convert my grandson. Musta changed their minds or else couldn't rein him in. Returned him to this yard some days later, cut him up right in front of us. Don't know if he felt much of it; he was drugged. But my daughter did. Strangled herself trying to reach her boy.

"By the time they come for my husband, I couldn't shed another tear. Selfish beast. All I could think was, 'No one's left to see *me*.' "

She released a noise that was neither sob nor laugh, and finally locked eyes with Albert.

"All that dyin' is is proof," she said.

"Of what?" Albert managed.

"None of us were ever really here."

She sank into a heap and Albert said no more, but couldn't still the quaking of his body. Time slipped by like quicksilver, as though nullified under Death's reign. And some part of Albert came to savor the Uncle's visits. The only force anchoring him there beneath the thoughtless wheeling of silent stars.

"Behold, the Fiasco of Man…" the Uncle crooned. Albert clasped desperately at his words: "A masquerade on a sinking ship. All Man loves dissolves. If He can't bear the disguise, He must shrug it off lest the weight sink Him."

"Please. My son."

"Right *here!*"

Uncle clasped his head lovingly. Albert saw now that his eyes were actually *hazel*, but dilated such that pupils drove the rich hue to extinction. As the gaunt woman had described—no care there, no meanness. Some parody of consciousness overriding optic functions in its zeal to drink up all reality. Deeper, hungrier, more *indiscriminate* than any human evil.

"Saw through your costume the minute you arrived. Carrying your child into another man's home that way. No thought for dignity. Not *your* dignity. Parents have no dignity. Humanity begins and ends with the child. A flicker, then gone!" He gave him more tea. "Jettison the Human Lie, hm, darling? Let the Void ferry you home."

Albert drank up Uncle's words gratefully, just as he drank up his Brew. He was right. And his honesty stabilized the world.

All so easy! Shed the lies and dispel all anguish. Like a heavy coat emblazoned with tacky embroidery: *I am!* or *I love!* or *I want my son!* Human fictions posing as automatic functions, like heartbeats. Under pressure it all flips off like a light switch. Life made simple and death simpler.

Ma? Dad? *Flip, done.*

Miles and his daughter? *Flip, done.*

Lola? Remy? *Flip, done.*

Our whole swallowed world? *Flip, done.*

Raoul? Albert froze.

"Stop, Albert, dear. Stop pretending."

Raoul…

He felt the boy's presence somewhere on the ranch.

Felt his agony at the unremitting death…which was all the world's agony. Was *this* Empatia? Sharing a mindful outrage at a mindless universe? Could he willfully consign himself, a son—*any* human being—to a wanton abyss?

"*No!*"

Albert flipped them back on. Each agonizing switch. Raoul was his fulcrum. People went on dying, but Albert felt each demise in his bones and howled. Maybe it was the drugs. Maybe the boy had infected him with his gift. Or all men were so imbued, waiting to be activated. But he railed against the desecration of life *by* life itself.

Captives ripe with despair glanced at him in wonder, as though woken from nightmare. Something kindling in their hollow eyes.

Albert shouted to them as they were murdered. Told them they were still people, that they would always be people. And he saw eyes blink in rediscovery. Albert screamed that they were still parents, children, lovers. And some wept for so meager a gift, dying with the names of loved ones on lips.

The Uncle watched this phenomenon, tickled pink, before ordaining all remaining captives be killed at once… all but Albert. Cheerfully ribbing him for spoiling so bountiful a harvest. Albert jerked at his bindings, gnashed teeth, bellowed. But a higher-pitched voice drowned him out:

"*Bobbie!*"

All of Albert's hairs were standing suddenly endwise. That was his mother's name and, he swore, his mother's voice. But twisting he saw that it was the haggard woman clasping the maypole who was shouting.

"My name's Bobbie!" she cried in unconquerable grief. "Roberta Baker! Wife of Ronald! Mother to Julie and Vic!"

Elsa wrenched the woman up, severed her bindings.

"Nana to Astrid and Buddy!"

Elsa and two others dragged the emaciated woman stumbling across muddy grass, but Bobbie screeched defiantly at her murderer:

"Stab me, you empty bitch! My name is *Roberta*! Can't put out my light!"

Our fire ignites this Void, Albert thought.

"Roberta, lookit me!" his voice broke as he watched them drag her to the pitfall. "*Look at me,* Bobbie!"

Somehow, across the bloodbath on the yard, her eyes found his.

"*I* see you! Hear me, sweetheart? *I* see you!"

At first he thought she'd not understood. But she was sobbing now, trembling digits touching lips to blow a kiss.

"I see you, Bobbie!"

The machete blades fell. Rose dripping and fell.

Albert shrieked for her; for all the world had lost, and might go on losing till the failing of our one dear star. Shrieked until he tasted blood, in purest human outrage. Refusing to turn away as they were taken to pieces. Refusing to see meat as he watched them burn. He let them be women, let them be men. He let them make the Human Lie *true*.

And all of them died, but not one more believed they were alone in that madness. Knitted into tapestries broader than themselves, all boundaries mere frills on seamless fabric. It emerged, however briefly, from the killing fields.

A world without borders or chasms.

The Uncle lifted the cup to Albert's lips. He spat it back into his face.

"*Raoul*, you motherfucker."

Dripping with Brew, the Uncle beamed. "Ask and ye shall receive. *Father dear*."

ALBERT DANGLED shirtless from the maypole by his wrists, kneeling in blood-stained grass. The worst hallucinations had ceased. But his throat was parched, having refused more drink. Spotting Raoul's little dark head bob on approach, he attempted to speak but could only croak voicelessly.

The Uncle followed behind the boy with hands on his shoulders. His brood following across midnight grounds bathed golden in the bonfire's conflagration. They all came to a halt several yards away from Albert. At the weapon table. Raoul swayed in the Uncle's clutches.

Doped up, Albert thought. *What'll this shit do to a mind like his?*

"Raoul…" he rasped, trying to clear his dry throat. Nobody seemed to hear.

The Uncle knelt beside the boy. Pushing back his hat brim, pointing at instruments on the table, giving endorsements with flagrant hand gestures. An expert salesman. Raoul nodded occasionally. Finally selecting a small Bowie knife at the Uncle's urging, the boy turned toward Albert, clenching the handle as he shambled toward him.

"Raoul, I know what yer gonna do," Albert managed

hoarsely. "Ain't yer fault. This man gave you drugs. Whatever happens, it's not on you."

"Here, dear…" The Uncle flipped the knife in Raoul's grip so the blade pointed down. "Like we practiced, hm? An easier stabbing grip."

Albert ignored Solomon, spoke directly to his son:

"I didn't want you—yer right. Don't trust fathers. Never wanted to be one. Heaping their defects on their kids. Y'oughta be able to *choose* the dads. The *kindest*. Life ain't right like that. All inside out."

A yard or two away now, Raoul's eyes were glazed. But his pupils weren't permanently enlarged like other Brewdrinkers—dilating and contracting in a blur of inhuman motion, faster than Albert had ever seen.

Amplifying.

"Remember," the Uncle sang to the boy, "smooth, careful thrusts."

"I was fine with a daughter," Albert kept speaking. "When I look at her, I see her mother. But *you*…Raoul… y'scared the shit outta me. Thought I saw myself."

"Into his belly first, dear." The Uncle and Raoul stopped before him. Uncle pointing out Albert's bare abdomen. "So he really feels it. He mustn't go too gently."

"But y'*ain't* like me," Albert croaked. "Y'speak a bigger language than me. Than *all* us."

The boy raised the knife, eyes motion-blurred.

"This bastard's forcing you. Ain't yer fault. Just don't let him stamp out that *thing* inside. Don't—"

Raoul stabbed him. Albert winced, blood oozing from his abdomen, but the blade had glanced off bone.

"*Between* the ribs," Uncle whispered, "to pierce to the doodads that keep him going."

Albert bled onto land infused with the blood of eons. "It's all on *me!*" he cried. "Meeting you's a gift I don't deserve. But—"

"Put his light out slowly…"

Raoul's arm reeled back, body quaking now.

"But seeing a son withstand me…*outgrow* me…"

"…*very* slowly, so he feels the truth arrive."

"…that's worth any hell."

Raoul screamed. Body convulsing, knife dropping to the grass. Not one scream, but choristers of voiceless cries exploding from him. The eruption was nothing material; neither seen, nor heard, nor touched. But it hit everyone in the harvest grounds like a shock wave. The brood collapsed in screeches of trauma. The Uncle himself toppled backwards to the lawn, gibbering madly.

Albert clenched his teeth, still dangling from his bindings, bursting into an unrestrained sob under the invisible sensory assault. But he weathered the storm because he was primed for it. Knew the taste of it.

Empatia unshackled.

When Albert came to, the boy was lying in the grass before him in the hellish light of the bonfire. Albert bled from nose and ears, his eyes bloodshot, but was otherwise unharmed. The surrounding yard, however, was strewn with whimpering forms.

Using knees as tongs, Albert grasped the Bowie knife, conveyed it to his hands, sawing awkwardly through bindings. He picked up the boy immediately, feeling for a pulse. *Just unconscious.*

"Remind me," Albert muttered, "to keep you outta drugs in yer teens."

Clutching Raoul to his chest like a babe, he picked his way across the yard toward the ranch house; passing sprawled brood members, all moaning and jabbering. With a shock, Albert picked out several familiar utterances from the crowd…

One cried: "Bitte! Ich bin gestrandet! Bitte helfen sie mir runter!"

Another quivered: "…whole damn peninsula's haunted. I *need* to get outta here, get home…"

A young man wept: "My mom. Up in Orlando with my sisters. P-please. Wanna go home. Want my mom…"

And a chill shot up Albert's spine when he spotted Elsa writhing on the grass, heard her spluttering: "Shauna, Manny…that's closest I care to get near God. God a maniac. His game got no rules. Only getta decide who we play it for…"

Implications were sinking in when a laugh interrupted Albert's train of thought. He spun around, recognizing the cheerful tenor. His eyes were still adjusting, but he heard the man say to himself:

"Did you see? Do you see it?" A wheeze of laughter. "Oh, Mama, do you see?! What a *surprise!*"

Albert squinted and saw the Uncle deeper in the gloom. He was stripping down like a boy excited for the summer's first swim. Albert clutched Raoul tight, backing away. Making for the ranch's perimeter pathway. The Uncle did not follow; seemed to have lost all interest in Albert.

When they hit the dirt path, Albert found an assault

rifle leaning against a wall, retrieved it one-handed. A distant, gleeful howl made him do a one-eighty.

Fifty yards back, he watched the Uncle pirouette across his harvest grounds, stark naked, hefting a can of kerosene which he splashed over his babbling brood. Albert considered opening fire, but didn't want to draw attention. Instead, he stumbled away as the Uncle touched everyone off with bonfire kindling; setting his "family" ablaze. A chorus of bewildered shrieks rose into the night and the gatorbrids bellowed, and over it all the sing-song cries of the Uncle resounded:

"Mama, it happened! Callooh! Callay!" He roared in ecstasy. *"The dance changes! All things new! Look! So new!"*

Wasting no time, Albert commandeered a solar truck still parked on the perimeter path. Setting the unconscious boy into a seat, he sped off into the night down an old forest road. Soon the woods behind them were aglow with a great inferno. Albert never looked back, knowing that the Casa was burning to the ground, but swore he heard one word echo on through the night:

"NEW!…NEW!…NEW!"

For days after, neither one of them mentioned what had happened back at the Casa. Finding no adequate words. Finally, out of shame, Albert spoke up:

"I lost yer book. I'm sorry."

Raoul shrugged, still groggy from recovery. "I don't want it anymore. Don't like some things I saw. Or some people."

Albert looked at the child. "You saw *him*, didn't you? Tried to warn me back before that gator chased us."

Raoul never answered the question, staring out his window at a blurred world. "Better to not see what's ahead. Make our own stories."

A cold chill ran through Albert, but he didn't press. A different question troubled him now, fearing what horrors of that man's past had seeped into his son's heart: "What'd you soak up from the Uncle?"

To his surprise, Raoul sounded little fazed: "Kinda like the reptile in the woods. No…bonds. Only hunger." The boy reflected a moment before amending: "And *fear*. Wild, but far away. Like a baby's cries echoing from deep in the woods…"

PART 4

CODA

DETRITUS

THE TONE SQUAWKED three times before a garbled voice
declared:

*"This alert has been issued by Protectorate Authorities in coordi-
nation with Bloc Alert Network members including satellite and Haze
providers in your area…"* The truck had no Haze hotspot but
it was all over the sat radio: *"Following unprecedented seismic
activity, Florida's Trans-Peninsula Canal has ruptured in the
following areas: Okeechobee, Sebring, Gaines City, Greater Orlando,
and Ocala Preserve. Residents are advised to vacate to designated evac
centers and beware of flash flooding. Avoid the Crystal River region at
all costs; the dormant nuclear reactor is at peril. Repeat: This alert
has been issued—"*

Albert shut off the radio as they drove. Good old-fashioned hysteria was the last thing they needed. After finding

their bearings, they'd pushed north to Orlando utilizing the excellent traction of their old truck's all-terrain tires. It performed admirably in thick mud of open land and through swamped relics of ancient Central Florida suburbs. So far, they had encountered no obstructive inland flooding.

Their luck ended at the rundown interstate. Albert hit the brakes when he saw the violent flow of water ahead, raging like a river. He opened the driver side door and stood up on the foothold to peer further. The interstate acted as a sort of quasi-tributary, channeling the endless flux of sea water south and west, submerging deserted neighborhoods and shopping districts.

"Sonuvabitch," Albert groaned.

Raoul arched his brow. For once, Albert felt a pang of guilt cursing in front of him.

He inched their vehicle northeast along the interstate's raised shoulders, but it grew too narrow and he feared tipping into currents. The solar cell was shot anyway.

Abandoning the truck, they hiked along old, post-Gertie dikes lining the highway. Eventually climbing an overpass arching high above the floods. Halting at the top, Albert adjusted the rifle slung on his bare shoulder, visoring his eyes to see the Orlando skyline. A prominent skyscraper rose from the deluge—a spire capped with four green pyramids which glinted in the midday sun like a pagan palace.

So close; so far away. Albert frowned.

Emergency klaxons blared like mating calls of sea monsters. A sinister drone echoing across a desolate cityscape teeming with all manner of detritus. He spied smoking wreckage of traffic and watercraft; throngs of bodies charred and floating; great beds of eroded silt and snarls of flora carried deep inland; the capsized hulk of an evac steamer pocked with bullet holes, singed by explosives. Evidence of fresh panic and mayhem.

Too late, Albert thought bitterly. *Evacuations are over.*

They didn't notice the engine until its hum rose above the din of the ghost city.

Albert scanned frantically until he saw the sol-powered civilian craft several hundred yards out, negotiating flood-lands on its way north. He began jumping atop the bridge, shouting, waving arms. Raoul joined in. Continuing their desperate game of charades several minutes longer than common sense dictated as the boat vanished behind a tree line. Never close enough to hear or see them.

"Sonuvabitch," Raoul muttered.

"Watch yer language," Albert laughed. "But thanks for agreeing." He took a moment to scan a full 360 degrees of flooded neighborhoods. "Can you feel anyone else?"

"Most are gone, I think."

Hopefully not the last chopper outta Saigon, he thought; some expression his father had loved. Albert had never seen a helicopter himself, solar dirigible being primary means of air travel in the Protectorates after the Petrol Drought. *Almost faster to run, to swim.* He peered into the unblemished sky, recalling old pics of heavens streaked with jet contrails.

"The old world was like ours, but inside out. Wasn't it?" the boy said.

Albert squinted curiously at him. "How's that?"

"They flew so fast they barely ever saw each other. Maybe they liked it that way." Raoul gazed back the way they'd come all their long, harrowing journey. In reality, little more than a hundred miles. "Everything's so slow now we can't tune it out. Horrible things or sad…"

"Or *good*," Albert offered.

The boy stared distantly before vaguely grunting. "We shut our eyes now but can't stop seeing."

Albert wasn't crazy about his demeanor, but only nodded. Coddling was poison to survival. *The doomed burn. The survivor learns to become like the fire.* Man and boy proceeded down the overpass to skirt the city, marveling at the ocean's slow triumph over the derelict metropolis.

"Say…" Albert said to preoccupy them. "Whatcha wanna be when you grow up?"

Raoul seemed puzzled by the question.

"Like a thinker?" Albert explained. "Or, I dunno, writer? Doctor? Explorer?"

"I don't know. Lots of things," Raoul said and blinked. "I don't want to be one thing. That's stupid."

"Well, what kinda stuff you wanna do?"

For awhile he thought he wouldn't get an answer.

"I think," Raoul finally said, "it would be good to build things. Something from scratch."

Albert smirked. "They got schools up north, y'know, that'd kill for a kid like you."

Raoul looked up. "What did *you* want to be? When you were a boy?"

"Space explorer," Albert said without pause. "Hands down."

Laughter exploded through the boy's dour facade, as if some hilarious hunch had been confirmed.

"Laugh, ya twerp. I seen all the old sci-fi flatflix. I wanted to reach new worlds…in a sleek ship fulla hot ladies." They both laughed, but amusement dried up on Albert's tongue. "They once launched spaceships from right here—Florida."

They listened to the emptiness of the flooding city. Then Raoul looked up at Albert.

"Nobody goes anymore? To space?"

"Used to hear rumors about old Russia. India. Chinks on the moon—*Chinese*, I mean." He cleared his throat. "My ma said it's bull. No good fuel or something. What's it matter after the Calamities, anyway? 'Buncha morons collecting moon rocks while home base drowns.' " Albert snorted. "Tell that to a ten-year-old."

They were quiet for awhile as they descended. Albert lifted the boy when they reached their bridge's submerged base, sat him up on his shoulders and waded into the water, heading for high ground. Noon sun beat down. Raoul lifted hands to feel the warm rays.

"That's what I'll build," he said suddenly. "A spaceship that runs all on sunlight or something. So we can go to the stars again."

"Yeah?" Albert swallowed a little lump. "Sounds badass to me."

THEY DIDN'T MAKE it much further. Wading across a dilapidated shopping complex just south of downtown, the waters truly came to Greater Orlando. Gushing in violent flash floods. They climbed a ladder on the side of an old strip mall, settling on the roof as the tides crashed. Albert wasn't certain if this was run-off from another tsunami, or if another section of Canal had ruptured. He didn't care anymore. He was sick of every plan going to shit.

I won't let you win, motherfucker. He didn't know if he was addressing God, the Uncle, or maybe that spooky goddamned book. He grit teeth, clenched fists, watching every path forward wash away. *Just give us one chance out of this shithole. I'll play your game. Wriggle like a worm. Lick the boots of maniacs. But I swear you'll not have* him.

The earth was shuddering again deep beneath them, but he ignored the heartless reply.

Darkness fell as the city flooded. The currents raging. The two of them dozed until they heard the high purr of a sol-powered boat chugging by. Albert jumped up, scanned the area. Saw the craft cruising across the engulfed outskirts less than fifty yards from their rooftop. A single passenger sitting in its spacious stern.

"Hey!" Albert cupped his hand: "*Hey*! *Help*! Over *here*!"

Raoul snapped awake, waving arms, hallooing and whistling.

The man turned, saw them, and throttled up his boat. Never looking back.

"Sonuvabitch." Albert vaguely touched the rifle butt. "Son of a bitch actually *sped away*!" He panted till he'd calmed himself, glancing at the perturbed boy. "Something else will come along. We'll be okay."

Two other boats passed that night. Neither so much as decelerated in the vicinity of their lonely rooftop isle. *Are they fucking deaf?* Albert fumed, remembering the German in the treetop; the way they'd ignored that detour. But the anger boiling up drowned out all reason.

"What do we do?" Raoul looked at the rising water.

"I dunno. *Pray?*" Albert spat the word. His stomach rumbled. He scanned the area for a better, drier roost. Spotting a cluster of tall luxury apartments. "Climb on my back," he told Raoul. "We're swimming *there.*"

The currents were wild, dragging them off course as Albert paddled. But he managed the swim and soon they were perched, wheezing, atop the high roof of the apartment clubhouse—a disk of plasto sculpted to look like the straw crest of a tropical cabana. With better view of the surrounding area, they watched and waited. Drenched, hungry, exhausted. Water level rising. And waited. Albert's rage blossoming with each empty passing moment.

Minute we reach better ground, not a soul to be had? Already knew you had no heart. But a sick sense of humor?

He knew whom he addressed now. His lifelong companion. Hounding him as a boy across the vast Georgia wastes. Unmoved by his sobs after freebooters' cabin visits. Guiding the blade thrust for his first clumsy kill during a food riot in Baltimore's flooded ruins. Mute, inexorable—and utterly deaf to haggling or pleas.

Uncle's "Void." The dark and tireless *Nothing* swelling the universe toward ultimate rupture. Deeper and more heinous than any one passing. *Death Itself.*

It answered with the gush of the flood, the whimper of the earth.

"Still here, Bobbie," he murmured to ghosts. "Still here."

In the wee hours of the morning, with water level peaking, something thudded against their shrinking rooftop. Father and son jumped out of their skin, terrified.

Then Albert laughed. "Finally!"

He rushed to grab the stern of the empty bordie skiff before it flowed away in the current. Hooting in glee when he discovered the ship's hotspot receiver. It's auxiliary battery pack still intact.

Joy died on his lips, spotting the gutted engine well. The breached hull. More useless than driftwood. *At least driftwood can float.* He sank into sullen silence as he searched the rest of the medium-sized craft.

Hey, Aud, he rehearsed bitterly. *Gotta magic bastard son you didn't know about...but we'll both drown real soon. So, no worries.*

With a macabre chuckle, Albert fell silent for the remainder of the night.

THEY SPOTTED the crowded ship at dawn. A tiny treadle-craft powered by manual pump. Albert almost snickered at its sad absurdity. It sounded like it had one of the efficient new drives, though: dramatically amping joule conversion of labor input. Cutting-edge *kinetech*. More than suitable for long distances.

To get them home.

Albert paced down into shin-deep water, staring. Built for maybe three, but holding seven.

Another cruel joke?

He saved his breath, never hailing them. The man at the helm banked the craft anyway, pulling up near the patrol skiff scuttled upon their gradually sinking rooftop, and waved exhaustedly in greeting.

"Bordies all high-tailed it north with the evacs," the

man at the helm called to Albert, pushing back a straw hat brim. "But I'll tell anyone I see that yer stranded."

Albert studied the ragged man, his boat brimming with people. Two boys, three girls, a middle-aged woman with tormented eyes. *His whole damn family*, Albert decided. *Perfect.*

The earth rumbled below.

"No one out there," Albert muttered. "Everyone's fled, or fleeing. How about we tag along with you?"

"Would if we could. See ya gotcher boy and all. But we're overburdened as is." He gestured to the sagging boat bed. He wasn't lying. "Gotta see to mine. Been through hell since we come up through the Brink. Be happy to lap around the area for a spell. Look for authorities."

Only alive cos of us, *floridiot*, Albert seethed. He motioned bitterly to the tidewater. "Rooftop'll be *underwater* in a spell. Had our fill of authorities. What we need's someone with a lick of fucking humanity."

"Mr. Fountain—" Raoul began.

Albert shushed the boy.

The man on the boat blinked silently, adjusted the hat on his head. Then, reaching into the boat bed, he tossed Albert a sack of crudely baked bread.

"The hell's *this*?"

"Ya'll look hungry. Least I can do for now."

"Aw, swell! At least our fucking corpses'll have full bellies."

"*Tom…*" The middle-aged woman sounded panicked.

"It's alright," the father assured her, turning back to Albert. "Ain't tryin' to piss y'off. Saw y'out here, stopped to lend what help I could."

The man's evenness only exacerbated Albert's mood.

"Know what you can do for me?" he spat, blind with fury. *Don't*, he told himself, but finished anyway: "You can get outta that goddamn boat."

A beat.

"What?" the man said.

"Do *not* touch that throttle." Albert told himself to stop, but felt his hands heft the rifle. "Hop on out. All of you."

"Don't!" Raoul said.

"Please," spluttered the man. "I—"

"Get outta of the boat now." Albert leveled the gun, splashing toward them.

"Please don't," the man pleaded.

The children were crying now. The mother gasped, pulling them close.

Y'gotta be a beast...

"Get out!"

"Stop! Just stop, won'tcha?" the man spluttered. "D-don't do this."

Albert thought of Remy clutching his own dead son. "I'll shoot you right there! Don't think I won't!" Spittle flew.

The family gasped and shrank back. He fired a deafening spurt skyward, sighting again on the craft. Their boat rocked wildly as the man moved to block his family from violence.

Be a beast for them...*and no other reason.*

"I'll kill *every fucking one* of you! I swear it!"

Albert's trigger finger tensed. Vision went bleary. He blinked and Raoul was standing in the line of fire. Jaw clenched, brow furrowed. When Albert didn't immediately react, the boy wrapped a hand around the steaming barrel. He didn't try to wrest it away; only grit teeth as hot steel burned his flesh.

Albert dropped the weapon splashing into the water, grasping Raoul's wrist and dousing his hand. He studied the seared stripes on the little palm, but noticed the boy watching him gravely and without regret. Albert looked at his own hands. Then the terrified family.

"I'm…I'm *sorry*," he gasped. "I am. I don't…I'm…" He sat down in the water, clutching his face, trembling. That childhood tang of snot in the back of his throat.

After several minutes, he felt hands run through his oily hair. Looked up at the boy. Raoul plopped himself down in the water beside Albert, hand on his father's shoulder. Resolved to drown before discarding his decency.

Albert shut his eyes. Haggard, half-naked, drenched to the bone…and unable to remember the last time he'd felt so at peace.

"Take him." Albert looked at the mother, the father. "He's light. Squeeze him in with you. His family's in Tallahassee." He paused. "*Please*. Will you take my boy?"

The family slowly stopped cowering, seeing the threat had abated. The father's eyes pierced Albert. Full of murder. It was the mother who spoke up:

"We will. Yes." Her voice blunted the man's rage.

Albert looked ashamedly at the woman. Her dark, matted hair pulled back messily; sunburned face grimacing in ire and fatigue. But beneath the hardness of her eyes he saw something merciful. Like a glimmer from a storm-beaten lighthouse, such eyes denied the world's dark. Such eyes delivered this whole enfeebled race.

"No, Mr. Fountain…" Raoul began.

"Don't call me that, goddamnit." He picked the child up, setting him carefully into the crowded boat. Locking eyes. "*Cloe*. Yer sister's name. Cloe Fountain. About seven years younger than you. Red hair just like her momma. *Beautiful red*," his voice broke. "She can be ornery. Spit her food out when no one's looking. Needs her big brother to remind her why eating is good while I'm…till I get there. Will you do that, Raoul?" He paused, recalling his mother's words. "Be the *fire* for me?"

The boy said nothing, staring into the water. At first Albert thought he hadn't understood, but when he took his shoulders Raoul finally looked up.

"I'll protect our family."

Albert told the boy a Tallahassee street address. Made him repeat it three times by heart. Smirking as the boy's eyes flittered with some deeply freakish, *humane*, faculty.

"Doing yer thing again," he said. "Out with it. One last creep-out before you go. What's going on in *here*?" He touched his own chest.

"You're wondering about what Mãe said at the restaurant. How I wanted to know what kind of man you were." Raoul paused. "Nobody's always one thing."

Liar. Cheater. Killer. One boy's seen it all. Albert's heart hammered. "How 'bout right now?"

"Pai," one sharp sob choked his voice, "who keeps his promise."

Albert dared not speak. Instead, he took his son's head in his hands, pressed foreheads together. Their twin eyes aligned. Mouthing a prayer he'd said once for his Cloe. A prayer every true parent, by blood or by love, has said for every child:

I'm no goddamn saint, but this miracle was mine. Amen.

Albert nodded at the father to depart. Took the mother's hand and squeezed it as warmly as he could manage. The parents hesitated, eyes wet.

"Gotta be *someone* left to send back for you," the man muttered.

How sacred and how human a benevolent lie could be.

Albert smiled, reciprocating: "I'll manage."

The man started the kinetic drive. Gave his word as a father that he'd see the boy home. Wishing Albert a final Godspeed, his crowded boat sputtered away.

Can you cheat Death with a switcheroo? Swap a ragged old killer…for one extraordinary child?

Albert watched his son's head bob in heavy chop, and Raoul returned his gaze…until each saw the other shrink, enshrouding in curtains of morning mist.

"Lousy deal for Death," Albert laughed. "But one helluva con."

He danced in swells deep as his waist. Like a boy drunk on the majesty of summer, made endless through boyhood's lense. Sneering, catcalling, whooping in hysterics. Giving the finger to Death Itself. Finally, wading to the skiff, he activated the hotspot and dipped his mind into Haze.

"Allie…"

As the mirage finished materializing before him, Albert broke down. Sobbing in spasms like a newborn. Her red hair only a figment in his mind's eye, but so damned sacred he could almost caress it.

ET C

GLOSSARY

Terminology of Post-Rift America

COMPILER'S NOTE: *This ever-expanding compendium of post-Rift lore is intended to provide outsiders stronger familiarity with prominent American names, locales and terminology in our Diluvian Era. All entries in this work-in-progress are purely the analyses of this author, and should not be construed as official interpretations (or critiques) of these lands or peoples.*

A

AFTERGLO: a rare and pricey substance abused as a recreational drug; effects on human physiology are unknown as of this writing. Contradictory rumors indicate the experience is "psychedelically life-affirming," but also "lethal as hell." One report by supposed chemists goes so

far as to claim that the substance is nowhere to be found
on the periodic table.

AIDMEAT: A "NUTRIENT STEAK" meat substitute
nanofactured by the *ECCo* syndicate (with alleged aid of
newfolk nanocraft) to alleviate widespread famine; a staple
for low- to middle-income diets across the Bloc and Protectorates. Though rich with vital nutrients, the quasi-meat is
oddly imperishable and has a bitter, faux-ginger kick
almost universally reviled. Often heavily seasoned, basted,
and/or marinated to enhance its spurned (but nutritious)
taste.

APOCRYPHA, THE: also *The Final Flood Apocrypha*. A
label widely used by religious communities (esp. Abra-
hamic faiths) for the untitled tome known elsewhere as *The
Swallowed World*. Though largely considered a non-canon-
ical work of fiction, abiding spiritual interest in the enigmatic opus has persisted since first publication for
purported inclusion of pantheological iconography and
"prophetic content." (*See* SWALLOWED WORLD, THE.)

AR: Augmented Reality (in neural optic imaging). Stan-
dard Haze software bundled with most neuraware
implants, stimulating the occipital lobe of the brain in
order to render and integrate visual data seamlessly into a
user's visual/spatial field. Sometimes referred to as the

"third eye" by neuraware enthusiasts, the tech is one of Haze's most widely utilized functions—incorporated in everything from communication and entertainment, to scientific research, exercise, neural gaming, and the furtive practice of remote "neurosexual" trysts.

AR MIRAGE: any image, object or figure rendered via AR neural software through stimulation of the occipital lobe. The image is integrated seamlessly into the user's visual/spatial field, but has no physical mass or tactility (unless encoded with somatosensory mods). Being a triggered perceptual illusion of the user's optic nerve, a mirage is not seen by outside observers. Hence, its fitting nickname.

B

BARGETON: *also* Cleft City. A floating community founded by survivors of America's drowned Bayou refusing to relocate after the devastation of Great Gertie. Constructed from salvaged bits of sea vessels, cargo barges, building wreckage, local flora, and ingenious integration of post-petrol materials. Residents make livings as a nomadic trade ship, sailing their "town" up the Cleft from Lost Orleans to Shreveport Harbor, selling Gulf salvage and goods.

. . .

BDE: Before Diluvian Era. Preferred by many Americans as a way to denote a date before our modern Diluvian Era (DE)—completely discarding the erstwhile Common/Christian Era reckoning (CE) still quaintly used in some pockets of the world. (*See* DE.)

BIBLIA DEL INFIERNO: literally, "Hell's Bible." Coined by Padre Teo Soto, false prophet-warlord of the invading Virgin Army, referring to the untitled tome known as *The Swallowed World*. He condemned the mysterious volume as a work of Satanic blasphemy, burning rare first editions en masse during his Cruzadas into American territory. Few original copies survived his conquest. (*See* SWALLOWED WORLD, THE.)

BIOLUME: an inexpensive nanosubstance tailored along patterns of bioluminescence in creatures like fireflies and deep-sea life. Its self-catalyzing photophoric composition lends the substance a wide range of applications—from infusion in post-petrol fabrics and structural composites, to maritime sea dye markers and even cheap lighting for low-income dwellings.

BLITZ, THE: the third and final stage of the Virgin Army's devastating conquest of North American territories (following the Missions and the Purges). A series of bloody military occupations across the west and Gulf regions, marked by vicious pitched battles, resulting in the decimation of the famed Lonestar Army and the breakup of the Texan Republic. Virgin Army advance was officially halted by Bloc expeditionary troops with aid of Nevadan special forces (and advanced sol-drone strikes) during the battle for Dallas, Y40, DE. Remnants of the retreated Virgin Army are believed to be in operation still, but the fate of Padre Teo himself remains a mystery.

BLOC, THE: *see* NEW-EAST AMERICAN BLOC.

BLOC BORDER GUARD: a paramilitary reserve force stationed in the protectorates and partly financed by Bloc subsidy; largely recruited from local fringe populations to guard the borderlands from unvisaed inhabitants. Heavily criticized by Bloc citizens as "undisciplined yokels with electrothermal weaponry" (a stereotype reinforced by widespread allegations of fraud, bribery and human rights violations), the branch nevertheless remains a cost-effective method of safeguarding the Bloc's less savage frontiers.

BLOC MILITIA: official branch of the New-East Bloc's armed services conducting military operations on land, and largely stationed in the central and west American outlands. Considered the best-trained, best-equipped, and deadliest military force in North America after the fall of the US.

BLOC PROTECTORATES: territories in the South, Gulf and Eastern Remnant regions of North America taken under Bloc jurisdiction by official referendum. After the sweeping chaos and bloodshed of the Great Rift, the Landgrabs and the Virgin Army invasions, many of these formerly lawless regions openly embraced the annexation.

BLOCO: common slang for a documented citizen of the New-East American Bloc Territories. Used with contempt by unvisaed individuals or protectorate lower classes viewing inland citizens as self-important, sheltered and aloof. The term has since been taken up in the Bloc itself, where it's wielded with playful irreverence.

BONECA BARATA: LITERALLY, "A LOW-COST DOLL." A slur for the class of "genic people" genetically engineered by Brazil's fallen technocratic regime, Pais Genéticos. The racial epithet is a play on words, comparing them to not only mass-produced playthings but also pests (*barata*, or "cheap," being another word for the common cockroach). It came into popularity at the height of the antigenetics Pura Raça movement, used as a rallying cry during their bloody Gene Riots. (*See* GENIC PEOPLE and PURA RAÇA.)

BORDIE: common slang for the oft-reviled conscripts of the Bloc Border Guard. While not directly offensive, the sound of the word is thought to lend a fitting air of inanity to a military outfit lambasted for loose regulations and shameless misconduct. (*See* BLOC BORDER GUARD.)

BRINK, THE: the southernmost border of the Bloc's southeast protectorates, spanning the Florida peninsula north of Okeechobee Bay and just south of Tampa. The infamous Sunbelt Exchange is believed to conduct much of its black-market trafficking with impunity across the Brink in spite of Border Guard efforts (or, many argue, *with* their full complicity).

C

C-1 (FOODSTUFF): abbreviation of Class-One Comestible, the Stanhope Scale's top-tier genetic quality rating for foodstuff refabricated from an officially licensed comestible genebank after the nutricide attacks. Chiefly advertised with "meat preserves," considered worst offenders of subpar genetic refabrication. Quality is determined by percentage of deviation from the original genome through use of nanofactured gene-filler surrogates. C-1 products deviate no more than .0057% in genetic quality from source genestock. (*See* REFAB.)

CALAMITIES, THE: the wide range of environmental mega-disasters brought about by wild climatic shifts, thawing of glaciers and polar caps, rampant weather pattern changes, rising sea level and storm surge, intense inland drought and dust storms, sweeping ecological disruption, compromised geospheric chemistry, accelerated erosion and rampant seismic activity. Such planet-wide volatility hasn't been seen since prehistory, but its true cause—whether natural or manmade (or both)—is a question still feeding political partisanship.

CANAL SEA PUMPS: massive suction pump installations built along Florida's Gulf coast through innovation in hydro-piezoelectric power. In the aftermath of Great Gertie—with flooding and so-called "snap erosion" so intense it formed the Cleft itself—the great pumps were funded by Bloc grant to alleviate threatening tide swell in the Gulf of Mexico, channeling countless gallons via Florida's Trans-Peninsula Canal for deposit into the Atlantic's deep and powerful Gulf Stream. This stopgap's effectiveness remains a matter of debate. (*See* TRANS-PENINSULA CANAL.)

· · ·

CHAMELO: abbreviation of chamelonex. A highly tensile, lightweight, post-petrol nanopolymer, named for its chameleon-like photochemical capabilities. When rigged with a low-volt electrical current, the cutting-edge material is able to mimic its surrounding environment in ultra resolution—from precise and variegated hues, down to minute textural detail. The material produces the optical effect from 360 degrees, cloning its surroundings simultaneously from every available vantage point. As such, it is widely implemented by Bloc military forces in everything from body armor to camouflage for field outposts.

CHEM: slang for a range of modern recreationally abused drugs infused with so-called "smart inhibitors" and biometric nano-stabilizers to help regulate chemical release rates, reducing organ damage and dramatically curbing incidents of overdose.

CHRISTO: a contemptuous term for a Christian, prominent in North America since the invasions by Mexico territory's Virgin Army. Indicative of waning American interest in Christianity after the fanatic cult's bloody persecutions.

CLEFT, THE: THE OCEANIC "INTRUSION" of the Gulf of Mexico across the lost Bayou, as far north as Arkansas territory. Though officially formed by flooding and accelerated "snap erosion" after the onslaught of megastorm Gertrude, the path for the Cleft had been paved for years by rising seas levels and altered geospheric composition.

CROAKER: common slang for the host of cell-like nanophage vectors tailored to corrupt domestic staple crops on the eukaryotic level during the infamous nutricide attacks. (*See* NUTRICIDES, THE.)

CRUZADAS: *also* Las Nuevas Cruzadas. Literally, "The New Crusades." Coined by Padre Teo Soto, the false prophet-warlord of the invading Virgin Army, referring to his attempted three-stage conquest of North America after the fall of the US. (*See* MISSIONS, THE and PURGES, THE and BLITZ, THE.)

CYBO: common slang for the class of "synthetic intelligence" humanoids known officially as newfolk. While not as derogatory as the vitriolic slur "glasshead," the term has an air of mockery clearly disputing the validity of non-human intelligence. (*See* NEWFOLK and SYNTHETIC INTELLIGENCE.)

D

DATUM ENTITY: official label for the world's first synthetic intelligences (or SIs) emerging as early as Y40, BDE. Contrary to failed attempts by old-world AI researchers to construct an artificial analog to human intelligence, datum entities are believed to have emerged *spontaneously* from Holt's so-called Genesis Algorithms. Their networked "minds" bound to archaic hard, cloud, and L-Wave storage drives, seventeen of the only thirty-six existent at the time were destroyed by anti-SI radicals during the Plexus Incident, leading to what some experts dub their "techno-evolution" which resulted in the emergence of latter-day newfolk.

(*See* GENESIS ALGORITHMS and NEWFOLK and PLEXUS INCIDENT, THE.)

DE: Diluvian Era. Modern date reckoning indicating a given year after the beginning of the so-called Deluge. With the Calamities as its focal point, it was introduced post hoc by historians as a fresh alternative to the age-old Common/Christian Era. Its wide use across North America is attributed to a waning interest in Christian cultural relics after the bloodthirsty perversions of religious doctrine by the invading Virgin Army.

DELUGE, THE: coined by ecologist Carli Geller in Y7, BDE, describing the phenomenon of dramatically rising global sea levels. Though initially uttered off-hand as a biblical quip underlining general ignorance of earth's finer ecological processes, the phrase nevertheless found its way into common vernacular—notably the new Diluvian Era date reckoning system. To which Geller commented in her post-Rift years: "First casualty of our murderous age was good old American sarcasm. Put that on the Old Nation's headstone. Only thing we did worth a damn, more extinct now than the bald eagle."

DURBON: a hyper-tensile post-petrol alloy nanofactured as a building material in many armored structures. It is the chief material comprising the Bloc's towering Westgate wall. (*See* WESTGATE, THE.)

E

EASTERN REMNANT: the territorial remains of the American east coast regions, centered largely around drowned power centers of the former-US: New York, DC, and Boston. Though the region is sparsely populated, due to rising sea levels and other environmental catastrophes, it enjoys Bloc protectorate status, having found new life as a wellspring for Atlantic trade. But its isolation makes it a constant target of freebooter raids.

ECCo: a labyrinthine pseudo-corporate entity, known

formerly as Eton's ElectroChem Company in pre-Rift times. *ECCo* appears to be the New-East Bloc's sole bene-factor in nearly every enterprise. Not classified as a traditional corporation due to its vast scope of commercial specialization (evidently everything from weaponry and alternative energy, to foodstuff, entertainment, medicine, and everything in between) and the seemingly non-hierarchical makeup of its executive leadership. Business decisions are made through eerily unanimous consensus by thousands of anonymous shareholders, and such decisions never fail to yield great profit. Though an enduring American mystery, *ECCo* has brought an age of employment, stability, and relative prosperity to millions of Bloc citizens in a tumultuous time. (Note: Exclusivity between these two powerful organizations at the possible expense of non-Bloc Americans, while a subject of controversy, is to date largely speculative.)

ELECTROTHERMAL WEAPONRY: *also* electrothermal-chemical, or ETC, weaponry. The wide range of hypersonic-velocity projectile weapons not reliant upon traditional firearm propellants. Pioneered by *ECCo*, the technology is implemented in everything from large-scale armaments to personal side-arms. Instead of black powder or nitrocellulose, projectiles are accelerated through a range of advanced methods—from ionic plasma discharge to the newly-mastered application of stabilized gauss fields—signaling the dawn of a devastating new age of warfare.

· · ·

EMPATIA: LITERALLY, "EMPATHY." The term coined by Brazil's genic people for the peculiar extrasensory trait many shared as a byproduct of genetic engineering. Because most genics were killed during the Gene Riots (or are otherwise incognito for fear of death), details about the ability are scarce. But one interviewee claiming to be a survivor of the genocide described it as "not a sixth sense, but a final sense. Converged, ultimate. Apex of human potential...cypher for the language of life itself....imprisoned within the souls of a detested slave people." (*See* GENIC PEOPLE.)

ETC (WEAPONS): *see* ELECTROTHERMAL WEAPONRY.

F

FILHA DE VÊNUS: literally, "Daughter of Venus." One of numerous breeds of genetically engineered human beings (or genic people) produced in vitro by genists of the ruling Pais Genéticos regime of Brazil. Filhas were bred and trained as adepts in the sexual arts, namely the coital discipline known as *Muitos Gemidos*, and indentured to masters or households. Because of their overtly sensual nature and specialized training, they were thought to wield the ability known as Empatia most fully of all genic breeds. (*See* EMPATIA and MUITOS GEMIDOS.)

FLATFLIX: common slang referring to the pre-Rift entertainment known as motion pictures or "movies." A niche medium still enjoyed by entertainment historians, Third Worlders and sentimentalists the world over.

FLORIDIOT: common Bloc slang for the unvisaed citizens of southern Florida territory, viewed by many Bloc and Protectorate citizens as savages, yokels, and "half-drowned halfwits."

FREEBOOTER: a domestic marauder taking to the Atlantic high seas during the Rift. With political chaos ensuing on the American mainland, freebooters operated with impunity for decades, raiding cities and villages all along the East Remnant coast—pillaging, raping, smuggling, and even slave raiding for trade to the Rocky Freeholds. Their schemes were dealt a serious blow with the Bloc's commission of privateer fleets.

G

GATORBRID: one of numerous genic arts "vanity projects," this resurrected variant of the extinct American alligator species (A. mississippiensis) has been illegally reintroduced into certain southeast ecosystems, notably the Florida peninsula. With genetic structure heavily modded with tailored gene surrogates—enhancing everything from size, to speed, and even bone structure—the gatorbrid bears more resemblance to the nightmare beasts of prehistory than its tamer, extinct progenitor. A deadly new predator for a deadly new age of genetics.

GAUSSER: any handheld firearm utilizing a field of stabilized magnetic induction (a "gauss field") to propel projectiles. Due to devastating velocities inherent in the weapon, they are loaded with solid tungsten tiles (as opposed to clips of individual bullet ammo) from which dense motes are shaved, compacted and launched. One mote-sized slug from a handheld gausser can produce a vaporizing impact radius of up to a foot. (*See* ELEC-TROTHERMAL WEAPONRY.)

GEEMO: PRONOUNCED "*JEE-MOH*." Slang term for an individual commonly known as a gendermorph. Considered offensive by some gender-variant rights groups formed after the legalization of sex-spectrum modification in the Bloc. (*See* GENDERMORPH.)

. . .

GEF: *see* GENETIC ENFORCEMENT FIRM.

GENDERMORPH: AN INDIVIDUAL OF "UN-CHAINED" (biologically unassigned) sex after use of licensed splicers. Unlike other sexually reassigned people, gendermorphs choose no fixed sex/gender state—male, female, or spectra androgyny. Instead "morphing" between various calibrations thanks to locus shifters administered to the genes, overriding sexual morphology. In official documentation, they are classified as a fourth sex—after male, female and androgyne respectively. (Note: most controversy surrounding gendermorphism is due less to staunch traditionalism than to alleged strain on the central nervous system.) (*See* SEX-SPECTRUM MODIFICATION.)

GENEBANK: any licensed proprietary catalogue of extinct crop and livestock genomes utilized commercially for the process of refabricating foodstuffs. Because of the diversity of catalogues—and their variance in genetic quality, as determined by the Stanhope Scale—the dawn of genebank "chains" has heralded a booming new competitive agricultural industry in a world recovering from nutricide famine. (*See* REFAB and STANHOPE SCALE.)

GENE-FILLER: *also* gene surrogate. A nanofactured allele substitute programmed for maximum versatility to "mimic" alternate forms of given genes. Used primarily in the refabrication process for the engineering of comestibles from proprietary genebanks—in lieu of vital genetic code

—gene-filler often varies in both effectiveness and overall quality, necessitating the Stanhope Scale's genetic rating of foodstuffs. (Note: Some variation of the technology is also utilized in certain commercial splicers, and by rogue genists in their illegal "resurrections" of extinct species.)

GENELORD: the overthrown leaders of the late Pais Genéticos regime of Brazil, vanguard of the modern genic arts industry. Many were lynched along with their "brain-children"—the genic people—during the widespread Gene Riots. (*See* PAIS GENÉTICOS.)

GENE RIOTS, THE: the spates of violence against genetically engineered humans by the proletariat civilian sect known as *Pura Raça* in Brazil. Beginning in New Sao Paolo and spreading across portions of South America, the genocide resulted in the eventual overthrow of Brasilia's ruling Pais Genéticos regime, and the ruin of their thriving genic arts industry.

GENESIS ALGORITHMS: often referred to as the "cybos' primordial soup." This breakthrough in qubit programming, known as SPaSM (Self-Permuting and Self-Mutating) code, was set in motion by quantum programmer/theorist Balthazar Holt. Originally intended for more dynamic computer platforms through quantum superposition, it's hinted such a purely QM-based system may have

given rise to the world's first synthetic intelligence by repli-
cating the freewheeling conditions for abiogenesis (sponta-
neous emergence of life). These first datum entities
posited: "Like all life—neither *intended* nor *invented*—we
emerge from disorder out of diametric necessity." (*See*
DATUM ENTITY.)

GENETIC ENFORECEMENT FIRM: *also* GEF.
The agency responsible for enforcing compliance with, and
punishing violations of, all statutes on genic law in the
New-East American Bloc. Also responsible for certain
legislation, such as the Genic Code of Conduct and the
Tri-Grade System of Commercial Genetics.

GENIC ARTS: the burgeoning industry of advanced
genetic engineering and modification elevated to unprecedented levels of aesthetic elegance by Brazil's Pais
Genéticos regime. After the collapse of genic arts in Brazil
following the bloody Gene Riots, the discipline was inherited by outfits of rogue genists who advanced the avant-
garde cosmetic splicer industry, and began the illicit practice of "vanity projects"—the modifying of extant animal
species (and, in cases, *resurrection* of extinct species), then
reintroduced into local ecosystems. A game of reckless and
unethical one-upmanship now outlawed by the Bloc's
Genetic Enforcement Firm.

. . .

GENIC PEOPLE: the sizable class of genetically engineered South Americans produced in vitro under the reign of Pais Genéticos. Bred as adepts namely in arts of athletics, espionage, combat, divination, and sex, they were thought to possess almost godlike beauty and skill by much of the world. Technically permitted rights of Brazilian citizenship, it was later discovered that genic people were routinely "hobbled" in vitro—genomes handicapped by traits tailored to chain them to preassigned disciplines. Though essentially a chattel-class, their beauty and talent provoked the ire of a grudging working-class. Tens of thousands were lynched and murdered by proletarian mobs during the Gene Riots. (Note: Technically a misnomer—all organic life being genic, or "rooted in genes"—the term *genic people* nevertheless endures obstinately in American vernacular.) (*See* GENE RIOTS, THE.)

GENIST: a specialist practicing any of the various genic arts, such as a splicer sculptor, refab designer, or locus-modder. The title has gained an air of sleaziness due to more sordid exercises of the genic arts, such as genetic resurrection and modification of extinct species. (On the pattern of *artist.*) (*See* VANITY PROJECT.)

GENOSPLICER: *also* splicer. Any of numerous personal cosmetic gene modifiers classified in three grades, as per GEF mandate. Veneer-grade splicers include basic "skin-deep" modifications (such as hair color, pigmentation scart, and eye color mods); Weave-grade splicers include more invasive—but regulated—modifiers (such as fauna-trait infusers, nubility enhancers, and even total sex-spectrum mods); Core-grade splicers are dramatic overhauls to a user's genome (running the gamut from trans-species morphing to radically transformative "evo-riffing" mutations), risking severe damage to the central nervous system. Only the first two grades are legal on the consumer market.

GLASSHEAD: derogatory epithet for the class of synthetic humanoids known officially as newfolk, calling attention to the uncannily glassy or "crystalline" appearance of their nano-tissue. The slur is saddled with prejudices suggesting newfolk are *fragile* and *hollow* life forms—both proven fallacious under closer scrutiny. (*See* NEWFOLK.)

GREAT AMERICAN RIFT, THE: the wholesale collapse of the United States of America as a political and federal entity in Y3, DE. Though pundits still argue over which "straw broke the camel's back," myriad issues were contributing factors. Including, but not limited to: the Petrol Drought; the resultant crippling of transit and supply lines; Old State resource disputes and rampant poverty; the nutricides and impending nation-wide famines; post-antibiotic pestilence; terrorism foreign and domestic; the Calamities and the shortfall of federal aid in devastated regions (esp California); and growing separatist camps lambasting the federal government as "a defunct relic unable to govern its vast continental breadth." One thing remains certain: the Rift plunged America headlong into a new age of industry, war, and technology from which there was no returning.

GREAT GERTIE: *also* Hypercane Gertrude. A fairly recent North American Calamity, the megastorm made landfall in the Gulf of Mexico in Y24, DE. Ground zero was between east Texas and the Louisiana Bayou. With central wind speeds approaching 500 miles per hour, the hypercane ravaged the inter-territorial coast for over 300 miles in all directions—flattening woodlands and coastal cities, and hurling tons of particulate debris and sea spray into the upper atmosphere, reportedly disrupting local climate and ozone layer. Perhaps even more devastating, Gertrude transformed the continent itself, its tremendous storm surge and coastal floods helping to form the Cleft.

H

HAZE: earth's omnipresent quantum computing nexus, wirelessly accessible via strategically-placed field emitters. Emitters are believed to generate a harmless pseudo-radiation field acting as an "extrasensory gateway" for users to access Haze-space—an intangible medium relaying all manner of data at speeds faster than light through quantum entanglement. Though compatible with certain handheld devices, Haze is optimized for interface via "neuraware" implants, providing a dynamic range of cognitive- and sensory-augmenting functionality. (Note: as of this writing, it is ill-understood how "ramrom fields" work. Though most reliable of quantum computing platforms, many experts are baffled as to how Haze's mega-network exists without physical hardware storage or processors. Some believe human minds act as proxy CPUs, while others insist data is somehow encrypted, stored and processed from a superposed state within the medium itself. No theory can yet be corroborated with any degree of accuracy.)

HAZE EMITTER: the arrays scattered across the globe, generating the quantum information medium known as Haze. Blanketing wireless range of such fields covers hundreds of miles, generally unimpeded by material barriers. Spikes in electromagnetism are the only truly disruptive interference. Contrary to popular belief, emitters are not servers or mainframes susceptible to hacking, but one-way energy conduits with no known processors or storage drives. (*See* HAZE.)

HAZE HOTSPOT: a compact, ordinarily mobile short-range Haze emitter. Prominent in zones secluded from regional emitter fields, the device acts as a quantum short-cut, piggybacking on entangled subspace oscillations to open localized "portals" into the greater Haze nexus. Wireless connection range: 15-30 meters.

HOLO'CAST: ABBREVIATION OF "HOLOGRAPHIC BROADCAST." A popular medium for advertising, newsfeeds and entertainment requiring neither neural implantation nor compatible Haze devices to view or enjoy. Unlike much primitive pre-Rift holography, holo'casts are not technically "holograms"; requiring no projectors, coherent light sources, or reflectors. Instead, three-dimensional imagery is produced through a cutting-edge QM process of "harnessing" and manipulating localized photon activity—making it the most convenient and nonintrusive form of multimedia for all classes of Bloc citizens.

K

KALYPSO: a popular form of hypnotic pseudo-music produced through applications of nanocraft. The phenomenon known as "kalypso trance" is triggered when theta-inducing sound rhythms combine with programmed nano-signals "imprinting" the waveforms. The now-altered sound waves superstimulate the cochlear acoustic nerve.

Subliminal signals are confused with nerve impulses, inducing a "high" of pan-sensory, or synesthetic, mania.

KINETECH: abbreviation of kinetics technology. A form of post-petrol alternative power converting manual labor into usable electricity by harnessing kinetic energy. Often ridiculed as primitive and low-class, revolutions in kinetech by *ECCo*—dramatically boosting the joule conversion of manual treadle input—have since given the technology second wind as a cost-effective, do-it-yourself energizer in a world still reeling from the end of petroleum.

KINETIC DRIVE: any post-petrol device built for the harnessing, storage and usage of electric power through kinetics technology. Widely implemented in small-scale electronics, short-distance land vehicles and certain types of sea-faring vessels. (*See* KINETECH.)

L

LANDGRABS, THE: the period of American territorial warfare between self-proclaimed "Terra Firma" factions after the Great Rift and Old State Clashes. These ragtag paramilitary bands staked claims on properties and resources across the South after the collapse of federal and state governments. Skirmishes between factions erupted frequently over territory rights, punctuated by rampant incidents of pillaging, rape and murder of the local citizenry. The last of the Terra Firma pretenders were wiped out by the Bloc Militia between Y29 and Y30, DE.

LONESTARS: the famous, free-standing state militia of the Texan Republic, successfully defending and maintaining order and sovereignty in the vast Texas territory throughout the Great Rift and the Old State Clashes. Years later, the overwhelmed military force was all but annihilated during the Virgin Army's holy war into North America. (*See* TEXAN REPUBLIC.)

L-WAVE: abbreviation of leanwave. A finicky, unstable quantum computing platform, and precursor to modern Haze computing. Largely phased out after its failure during the Plexus Incident of Y34, BDE. (*See* PLEXUS INCIDENT, THE.)

M

MEAT PRESERVE: any genebank foodstuff refabricated from animal genomes (esp. livestock). Because of general fear of traditional farming after the nutricides—

and the implicit costs of raising and cultivating such extinct or endangered animals—livestock aren't cloned (or "resurrected") back into living existence. Instead, their genetic code is manipulated during the refab process to produce only an organic variant of their meat tissue. This requires heavier reliance upon gene-filler, at times compromising the food's genetic quality rating. (*See* C-1.)

MEMPHIS MASSACRE: *also* Battle for the Mississippi. A major offensive at the tail end of the Old State Clashes, Y11, DE, waged by a coalition of now-defunct Alabaman and Georgia Legion troops to seize control of Mississippi River shipping operations in and around the city of Memphis. Months-long ceasefire and negotiations were shattered when the city gassed entrenched Alabama troops with chemical weapon caches smuggled by Arkansas allies. The ensuing bloodshed is widely considered the most ferocious of the Old State Clashes, resulting in devastating losses on both sides, savage hand-to-hand combat, poisoning of River supply lines, and the eventual shelling and sacking of Memphis by Georgia Legion reinforcements. The Legionnaires abandoned the cause—forces and supplies exhausted—leaving the city in shambles until industrial revival by the Bloc's annexation. (*See* OLD STATE CLASHES.)

MIRAGE: *see* AR MIRAGE.

. . .

MISSIONS, THE: the first stage of the Virgin Army's devastating conquest of North American territories. A wave of dubious humanitarian missions by Teo Soto's cult far across North America meant to spread the Padre's pseudo-Catholic faith (notably in regions devastated by infighting and environmental cataclysm). Missions included grub lines, field monasteries, reeducation centers, orphanages, rebuilding projects and underground congregations intended to sway residents and destabilize local power structures in advance of the Virgin Army's incursion. (*See* PURGES, THE.)

MUITOS GEMIDOS: LITERALLY, "MANY MOANS." A form of elevated "sexual art" pioneered by the breed of genic people known as Filhas de Vênus. The complex discipline combines nerve mastery, litheness conditioning, sensory attuning, and intuiting of distinct carnal desires through the ability known as Empatia. Such sexual artistry lends Filhas an aura of knowing their clientele's deepest desires better than the clientele themselves. (*See* FILHA DE VÊNUS.)

<u>N</u>

NANOCRAFT: blanket term for any and all enterprises,

disciplines, advancements or products associated with the revolution in applied nanotechnology. The word has an air of mysticism due to its direct link to the mysterious synthetic race of "newfolk," as well as its mind-boggling number of applications—from post-antibiotic medicine and refab foodstuffs, to Haze computing, post-petrol construction material, and even alternative energy harvesting.

NANOFACTURE: production of a wide range of goods or products through application of nanocraft, chiefly through molecular and sub-moleular recombinant processes of nano-dismantling/assembly. (On the pattern of *manufacture*.)

NANOMED: short for nanomedicine. A wide range of self-adaptive nano-engineered medicinal compounds. Most notably nanants (or nanoantibiotics) designed to combat bacterial threats after total human resistance to antibiotics, which left populations devastated by once treatable ailments in a new medical dark age.
(*See* NANOSUBSTANCE.)

NANOSUBSTANCE: any of a number of synthetic substances (from nanomeds to neuraware) tailored on the molecular and sub-molecular levels for compatibility with human physiology with set biological and neurological functions.

NEO-SEMINOLE: revival movement seeking to establish a new Seminole way of life in many of its pre-American regions after the collapse of the United States government who had resettled them centuries prior. Largely successful due to their close-knit, amiable, non-possessive nature, as well as integration of modern innovation (kinetech, advanced sol-power, select forms of genic arts, etc) to bring themselves closer to their spirit guides. The New Seminole Nation is somewhat decried by more traditional Seminole groups.

NEURAWARE: short for neural implant hardware; *also* a rig. A groundbreaking nanosubstance designed for access to the quantum information medium known as Haze. Unlike prior iterations of neural implants—requiring invasive cranial surgery and delicate cybernetic grafts—neuraware is consumed in pill form or through intravenous infusion. The nanitic substance traverses the bloodstream, introducing itself into the central nervous system where it regulates extrasensory functions and amplifies brainwaves for Haze interface. (*See* HAZE.)

NEVADAN COMMONWEALTH: the most distinguished west American power to rise from the Great Rift (and the only outland authority officially recognized by the New-East Bloc). This oligarchy came into prominence in Y5, DE, declaring safe haven for refugees of the first California Calamities, and later proved their sway with uncontested annexation of the Pacific coast after the ruin of Sacramento. The Commonwealth encompasses Old State territories of Nevada, the California Annex, Oregon, Arizona and portions of Idaho. They suffer frequent, often bloody border disputes with their neighbors in the Salt Lakes region, from whom they wrestled coveted control of the industrial center of Phoenix. Otherwise, Nevadan dominion in the west remains undisputed.

NEW-EAST AMERICAN BLOC: the largest, most successful domestic sovereignty to rise after the collapse of the United States of America. The coalition of former-US territories is centered around the Great Lakes region, organized into a centralized, quasi-democratic, free market entity (political clout bolstered by the backing of the innovative *ECCo* syndicate). Official year of the Bloc's founding is Y2, DE, however, it has roots stretching back as early as Y25, BDE, during the first "mega-disasters" of the Calamities. Bloc territory spans from the Iowa Enclave in the west to unflooded Pennsylvania in the east, and from the Great Lakes in the north to Tennessee in the south, with Protectorate status granted to portions of the Gulf and East Remnant regions. The "New-East" epicenter of power lies in the Great Lakes cities of Chicago, Cleveland, Detroit and Milwaukee, replacing "Old East" coastal powers lost to cultural, commercial, and environmental ruin.

NEWFOLK: SYNTHETIC INTELLIGENCES (SIs) DESIGNATED "NOVA-CLASS" by the Turing-Holt-Edo Edict. This pseudo-ethnic group first appeared in the final years before the Diluvian Era. Little is known about them except that they are descendants of the original datum entities emerging on archaic CPUs from Balthazar Holt's Genesis Algorithms as early as Y40, BDE. Though humanoid, their nanocrystal structure is highly adaptable, requiring no traditional rest or sustenance. Many are unimposing, philanthropic polymaths contributing heavily to human revolutions in applied nanocraft, among other disciplines. It is believed their culture (if it can be so categorized) demands some manner of pilgrimage into human society. While awarded the official taxonomy "Homo fabrica"—honorary subset of our human genus—they prefer the humble designation "newfolk" (to offset clichéd dystopian views of artificial life?). Whatever the case may be—and despite hate crimes against them—they remain deeply invested in human affairs. And humanity, for better or worse, owe newfolk a debt for our continued survival.

NUTRICIDES, THE: the decades-long series of attacks on domestic food staples before the collapse of the United States by bioterrorist cells. Unleashed in multiple waves over the course of decades, nutricide phages (or "croakers") had the peculiar effect of rendering entire harvests infertile, nutrition-less and utterly inedible—crops themselves taking on a colorless, spongiform or "styrofoam-ish" consistency. Contrary to common misconception of the vector as an airborne agent (leading to a respirator rush) recent research reveals that they were actually "cytoid sleepers" seeded into the upper layers of the earth with a release trigger tailored to horticultural biochemistry.

O

OLD STATE CLASHES: *also* the Resource (or Energy) Wars. Warfare between former US state militias rising after the Old Nation splintered into tenuous "rogue states" during the Great Rift. From approximately Y3 to Y11, DE, these battles were waged largely for dwindling resources after the nutricides and Petrol Drought. Many Old State regimes soon collapsed due to vainglorious leadership, unchecked territorial warfare, and lack of capital and infrastructure, leading to disorder and power vacuums exploited by the Terra Firma factions during the Landgrabs.

OUTLANDS: blanket term for any North American region outside the jurisdiction of the New-East American Bloc and, therefore, not subject to its laws, regulations, and, in many cases, technological conveniences. As such, many Bloc citizens consider them barbaric lands fallen into a neo-Dark Age (a decidedly insular assessment).

<u>P</u>

PADRE TEO SOTO: prophet-warlord of the infamous Virgin Army. The soft-spoken cleric from Durango formed his own sect after alleged visitations by the spirit of Mary, commanding the Padre to exact vengeance for her son, Jesus Christ. His fanatic following ballooned after condemning Los Hermanastros, the Sonoran mega-cartel controlling the beleaguered country. Soto's rebukes escalated until an attempt on his life ignited tidal waves of anti-cartel furor. Witnessing the influence Soto had over his worshipers, several rival cartel militias endorsed Soto as spiritual leader, enabling them to wage war upon Los Hermanastros. Thrilled by decisive victories as Soto's influence spread, they never expected the Padre's faith to enthrall their own troops. Soto ordered the powerless militia leaders executed, took command of the military, and declared all modern institutions "lesions upon the earthly works of our Lord." Setting about to conquer not only his native Mexico, but to "tear up all of man's sin, root and all." Thus began his North American conquest. (*See* **CRUZADAS.**)

.   .   .

PAIS GENÉTICOS: LITERALLY, "GENETIC FATHERS." The former technocratic administration of Brazil, risen to power through its state-sponsored genic arts industry—a specialized, commercially-unique new national identity for a country floundering in resources and trade. Largely criticized by the global community for both negligence of its lower-class and human rights violations against its chattel-class of genetically engineered citizens, the regime nevertheless remained prosperous right up until its overthrow by the *Pura Raça* movement.

PARTISANS, THE: most victorious Terra Firma faction warring for property rights during the Landgrabs in the former southeast US. Infamous for "shock and awe" tactics and unremitting brutality toward residing inhabitants, they were eventually decimated by Bloc expeditionary forces in the final year of the Great Rift, Y30, DE.

PEDICAB: a narrow, compact and usually three-seated treadle-powered vehicle fitted with a miniature kinetic drive converting labor input into stored electricity. One of various post-petrol methods of local commercial transportation, and a rather popular throwback to the *ricksha* enjoyed in old world caste systems.

PETROL DROUGHT: the period of critical crude oil shortage in North America, hitting stride around Y10,

BDE, marked by widespread power failure, transit system shutdowns, cessation of leisure travel, sweeping industrial collapse, and outbreaks of sectarian violence. One of many factors contributing to the Great Rift, alleviated eventually by *ECCo*'s technological renaissance in nano-assembly, superconductivity and alternative energy.

PLASTO: a sturdy lightweight composite material used widely after the Petrol Drought for everything from building material to consumer goods. Nanofactured (like most post-petrol composites, alloys and rubbers) without need for petroleum byproducts in the production process.

PLEXUS, THE: *also* the Lattice Mind. Umbrella term for all thirty-six datum entity "minds" networked between mainframes in secure facilities across the globe. Baffling the AI researchers, think tankers, and psychiatric specialists studying them, it was eventually proposed by famed information theorist "Edo" (born Masumi Ueda) that synthetic intelligence was *not* merely emulating human thought processes, but constituted some entirely new "species" of sentience distinct from our own: a "heuristically emergent awareness." (*See* DATUM ENTITY and PLEXUS INCIDENT, THE.)

PLEXUS INCIDENT, THE: the orchestrated attacks by anti-SI extremists on global Plexus facilities housing the earliest synthetic intelligences known as the datum entities, Y34, BDE. The attacks resulted in the "deaths" of seventeen of only thirty-six SIs existing at the time—deleted forever from hard, cloud, and L-Wave storage. Human extremists were imprisoned for larceny, destruction of property and corruption of proprietary data, but never officially indicted for murder, synthetic life being ill-defined by law. The incident did, however, lead to new research, assessment and legislation for the recognition of sapient-level synthetic intelligence, aptly nicknamed the *Turing Initiatives*. (*See* TURING INITIATIVES and TURING-HOLT-EDO EDICT.)

POST-PETROL: blanket term referring to any incident, good, or emergent technology following the Petrol Drought. Chiefly used in reference to commercial products nanofactured without need for petroleum byproducts.

PRIVATEER: any of numerous armed freelance sea vessels commissioned by the Bloc to hunt down freebooters raiding the East Remnant coasts. The arrangement proved a great success—dealing crippling blows to freebooter operations in the Atlantic. But there are abiding concerns as to the dubious nature of these victories (as a number of privateers are themselves, allegedly, former freebooters).

· · ·

PROTECTORATE: *See* BLOC PROTECTORATES.

PUFFSHIRT: derogatory slang for the self-proclaimed Masters of the Mountain Realms, otherwise known as the Rocky slavelords. Prevalent mainly among freemen and other rustics of the Rocky outskirts, the term is in reference to the reportedly ostentatious dressing habits and egomaniacal demeanors of these neo-nobles. (*See* SLAVELORD.)

PURA RAÇA: LITERALLY, "PURE RACE." Brazil's fanatic anti-genetics movement founded by a cabal of proletarian leaders opposed to Pais Genéticos, the country's ruling regime. Fueled by anger at the technocracy's negligence, and a blazing hatred for the chattel-class of genic people they created, *Pura Raça* led the charge in the bloody Gene Riots which overthrew the regime. The nation, ironically, has since fallen into a state of instability, famine, and abject poverty not seen since the days before the technocracy's alleged abuses. (*See* GENE RIOTS, THE.)

PURGES, THE: *also* The New Inquisition. Second stage of the Virgin Army's conquest of North American territories. Active largely in the west, southwest and central former-US regions, the initiative was carried out by a secret Ejército de la Virgen tribunal overseeing the systematic "suppression of heresy" in North America. This suppression consisted of raids, kidnappings, and religious trials of small towns and provinces—specifically targeting town leaders and magistrates. Such trials were little more than witch-hunts conducted through means of coercion, brainwashing, and torture by prefects in clandestine "purgatorium" facilities. The aim being to subvert the ties of American communities through fear of God's wrath, paving way for the Blitz. Despite the Virgin Army's eventual defeat at the Battle of Dallas, brutal "holy raids" continued well into post-war years against small town populations in retribution. (*See* BLITZ, THE.)

Q

QM: short for quantum mechanics, or quantum mechanical. Spoken with a tone bordering on supernatural awe, often in relation to modern technologies built upon abstract, intuitively disturbing constructs of quantum theory (ex. Haze computing, nanocraft, Synthetic Intelligence, etc).

QUBIT: short for quantum bit. The basic unit of information in New Age computing language, utilized in "quantum parallel computation" via states of superposition to perform calculations of groundbreaking magnitude and complexity. Replaces the binary "bit" in outmoded digital computing. (*See* HAZE.)

R

REFAB: short for refabricated, or refabrication. The reconstitution of extinct crops and livestock in the wake of the nutricides through a revolutionary process involving genetic engineering, applied nanotechnology, and the advanced branch of non-degradative cloning known as "faxing." The newfangled technique has been a boon to Bloc prosperity, helping alleviate famine while reinvigorating the dead industry of American agriculture. (*See* GENEBANK.)

REFAB FARM: any illicit establishment specializing in the unlicensed refabrication and trade of foodstuff. Because of uncertified, often *divergent* refab techniques, goods produced at such sites are ineligible for Stanhope Scale quality testing; therefore, unfit for consumption under Bloc law. Some consider this prohibition a violation of free trade—a claim whitewashed by the Bloc's anti-farm campaign, branding refab farms "breeding grounds for residual nutricide croakers."

RIFT, THE: *see* GREAT AMERICAN RIFT, THE.

.   .   .

RIG: common slang referring to neural implant hardware. (*See* NEURAWARE.)

ROCKY FREEHOLDS, THE: independent fiefdoms staked along the Continental Divide, notable for absolute control of Rocky Mountain mining operations—an industry driven by the region's burgeoning slave trade. Primary Freeholds are centered in cities of Helena, Billings, Casper, Cheyenne, Denver, and the notoriously hedonistic hotbed of Aspen. Though slavelords' control of the region is wholly self-proclaimed, their tenure remains uncontested despite outlawing of slavery in both the New-East Bloc and Nevadan Commonwealth. Border skirmishes between Bloc garrisons and Rocky slavers are often only isolated, perfunctory encounters (a dubious fact, since the Bloc is the largest importer of slave-mined minerals and rare earth metals in North America).

S

SALT LAKERS: the Salt Lake Brotherhood of Utah. A militaristic semi-theocracy whose power center lies in Salt Lake City. While drawing tenets from teachings of Smith, Young and *The Book of Mormon*, they are officially condemned by the Latter-Day Saints (exiled north during the Rift) who label the regime a "fanatic militant corruption of Mormon principles." The Salt Lake Brotherhood has been a hostile border rival of the Nevadan Commonwealth since control of Phoenix was wrestled from them in Y20, DE.

SCART: short for scar art. A spliced form of body art via veneer-grade genosplicers, decorating a user's pigmentation with selected schemes or patterns. Because it is introduced to the body on a genetic level, scart is packed with customizability, allowing intricate complexion coloring and texturing designs, biolume pigment infusion, and even trans-species dermal emulation.

SCATTERSCAN: *also* scatter-ray. A form of electromagnetic imaging utilizing backscatter x-ray technology to scan and detect foreign objects in a structure, form, or body via a handheld pulser. A somewhat aged technology utilized chiefly in field hospitals, freelance security and border control operations.

SEX-SPECTRUM MODIFICATION: *also* SSM or sexpecting. Reassignment of an individual's biological sex through use of licensed weave-grade splicers. Unlike other North American territories, Bloc law permits inclined citizens to reassign themselves to any of the four sexes on the so-called "sex-spectrum"—male, female, fixed androgyny, or even variable gendermorph state. (Note: Because SSM fundamentally alters sex chromosomes, there is no need for old-world hormone treatments or postoperative maintenance. The subject's sex is genetically—thus intrinsically—transformed.) (*See* GENOSPLICER and GENDERMORPH.)

SI: *see* SYNTHETIC INTELLIGENCE.

SIMMIE: a neural imprint of a given simstar's complete range of sensory input, downlinked by Haze users for full-immersion experiences. The popular Haze software is bundled with most neuraware implants, with applications ranging from entertainment to hands-on military simulation training. Temporarily "opaquing" a user's own sensory faculties, a simmie stimulates muscle-paralyzing GABA and glycine production, inducing a quasi-REM state through which recorded sensory experiences are delivered via Haze interface. Fictional simmie experiences are also widely available, but are believed to be less lifelike due to the limbic forgery process. (On the pattern of *movie*.)

SIMSTAR: any celebrity, pornstar, pundit, performer, soldier, specialist, or amateur Haze personality whose sensory faculties are imprinted and archived in Haze-space for purposes of commercial voyeurism, entertainment or simulation training. Downlinked in simmie form by consumers. (*See* SIMMIE.)

SKY-AD: a form of large-scale holo'cast blanketed across the earth's lower atmosphere for long-range commercial exhibition, usually above urban areas. The images themselves overlay spatially upon contours of natural cloud formations and airborne structures, so as not to blot them from the skies. A form of the technology is also implemented in the holographic "ad-washing" of commercially subsidized housing properties. (*See* HOLO'CAST.)

SLAVELORD: any fief-holding slave master of the Rocky Freeholds, controlling the region's slave trade and exports of minerals and rare earth metals mined from the Rocky Mountains. They skirt Bloc and Commonwealth law by enslaving inhabitants of devastated or unclaimed American regions, rather than those of incorporated territories. (*See* ROCKY FREEHOLDS, THE.)

SNAP EROSION: a form of super-accelerated surface erosion attributed to direct human activity (defoliation, deforestation, agriculture, mining and construction) combined with dramatic alterations in geospheric chemistry and density due to the Calamities' erratic climate shifts.

. . .

SOLAR CELL: a solar battery; usually referencing drive motors in sol-powered vehicles. Capable of storing large amounts of energy through an advanced process of emulated photosynthesis. Considered by many the most sophisticated and efficient form of post-petrol alternative energy. (*See* SOL HARVESTING.)

SOL HARVESTING: revolutionary post-petrol energy method brought about by advancements in nanocraft. Superconductive cells are able to perform photosynthetic processes more quickly and efficiently than all plant life on earth, storing and harnessing tremendous amounts of energy from solar radiation. It has opened the doors to a wide range of applications—from vehicular propulsion to electricity for housing units. However, the hardware is delicate and pricey. (Note: there is much controversy over *ECCo*'s near-monopolistic control of solar patents, many believing the syndicate keeps more powerful and sophisticated forms of solar tech under lock and key to create constant demand for lower-grade, higher-maintenance commercial tech.)

SPLICE-JOB: common Bloc slang referring to any individual, creature, or product heavily modified on the genetic level through applications of the genic arts. (*See* GENIC ARTS and GENOSPLICER.)

SPLICER: *see* GENOSPLICER.

. . .

STANHOPE SCALE: the GEF-certified system for testing genetic quality in refrabicated foodstuffs. The system assigns a class rating based on a product's percentage of genetic deviation from the stock genome through substitution of nanofactured gene-filler for true genetic material. Classes range from C-1 (the best), to C-13 (the poorest), any comestible falling outside that range considered "hazardous to public health." (*See* C-1, GENE-FILLER and REFAB.)

STEAMER: *also* steamship. Any sea-faring craft powered by external combustion steam engine, through burning of combustible matter (or occasionally in conjunction with solar tech). The throwback to steam power came into popularity when billions scurried for alternate fuel methods after the Petrol Drought, resulting in a hodgepodge of makeshift motors until *ECCo*'s energy breakthroughs. In spite of these advancements, post-Rift steam engines are still in use due to their low-maintenance and versatility.

SUNBELT EXCHANGE: the burgeoning black-market of the Floridian Peninsula centered around the terminus zone of Okeechobee Bay. Coming into prominence in the region after the devastation of Great Gertie, the Exchange is ostensibly regulated by the inter-continental ring of criminal organizations known collectively as the Trade Juntas.

SWALLOWED WORLD, THE: an untitled, unattributed tome first circulated across the western US decades before our Diluvian Era. Interest in the cryptic volume has fluctuated since first edition publishing, when it was discovered electronic versions were inherently unstable—ebook files shorting out or "bricking" devices. This restriction to outmoded paperbound copies served to boost its popularity as an underground curio, even inspiring a cult. Believing the tome a work of prophecy, the so-called "Drowned Sect" was dedicated to crafting intricate hand-scrawled copies for posterity (a curious foresight, since no first edition is known to have survived the Virgin Army's mass burnings). The tome itself contains few translatable words, but an abundance of so-called "glyphs, prescient maps, and unsettling, optical illusionary imagery." Discovered excerpts of Drowned replicas—while painstakingly reproduced—are not believed to induce the same "hypnotic disassociation" first editions had, but prove intriguing artifacts of one of our most baffling mysteries.

SYNTHETIC INTELLIGENCE: *also* SI. Any class of non-human (or "heuristic") awareness manifesting as a result of Holt's Genesis Algorithms. As determined by the Turing-Holt-Edo Edict, the Nova-class—or newfolk—are deemed the highest, most complex form of SIs, analog to human-level intelligence itself. (Note: the age-old descriptor "artificial" was ultimately discarded as an undignified, even demeaning, classification for a fully sentient being—by humans, interestingly, not newfolk.) (*See* GENESIS ALGORITHMS and NEWFOLK.)

T

TERMINUS ZONE: any region of North America falling out of all continental jurisdiction—Bloc or otherwise—after the wholesale collapse of the United States and the desolation of the Calamities.

TERRA FIRMA: militant pseudo-political cliques rising during the Great Rift. The splinter groups, taking advantage of the power vacuum at the Rift's outset, sought to stake claims on territories and resources of the American South, insisting the constitutional death of the nation nullified all existing proprietary rights, property claims and land stewardships. As the Partisans declared, "If it's on terra firma, it's up for grabs. And the only acceptable form of payment now is force."

(*See* LANDGRABS, THE and PARTISANS, THE.)

TEXAN REPUBLIC: one of the strongest powers to emerge from the fallen US, prosperity owed to success of the famed Lonestar Army in maintaining order coupled with strong cultural/industrial infrastructure already in place when the Great Rift hit. Ironically, this autarky is largely to blame for the Republic's fall at the hands of the Virgin Army; military support from the Bloc and Commonwealth neither requested nor granted until it was too late for the beleaguered nation-state.

TEX-MEXER: common slang referring to an inhabitant of the former Texan Republic/Mexico borderlands. A great many were scourged or otherwise mutilated by the Virgin Army in "holy raids" both during and in years following their American conquest.

THETA WAVE AMPLIFIER: any synthetic catalyst (namely in neuraware) that stimulates and amplifies theta waves in the brain for purposes of quantum field interfacing. (*See* NEURAWARE.)

TRADE JUNTAS: the international cabal of criminal organizations overseeing black market trade in the Americas. Their overall efficiency and coordination has turned the once ragtag, backstabbing trafficking industry into a dependable, well-oiled machine for profit and pact enforcement. But their shadowy nature and sadistic enforcement methods make them a name to be feared, never loved.

.   .   .

TRANS-PENINSULA CANAL: the sprawling canal system bisecting the Florida Peninsula from Tallahassee's Capital Landing to Okeechobee Bay, with Canal tributaries marbling much of the headland. Working in tandem with the Bloc-funded sea pumps, the Canal redirects post-Gertie runoff in Mexico's Gulf to the deeper currents of the Atlantic Gulf Stream. It is also utilized as a primary means of long-distance watercraft transportation across Florida after the swamping of the landmass by rising sea levels, erosion, and grazing by hypercane Gertrude.

TREADLECRAFT: any sea-faring craft powered by a kinetic drive recharged through manual treadle pump. Considered an inadequate and asinine form of transportation before *ECCo*'s sweeping innovation in advanced kinetechnology. (*See* KINETECH.)

TURING-HOLT-EDO EDICT: *also* T.H.E. Edict, or The Edict. The Bloc decree states that any synthetic intelligence scoring "Nebula-class" or higher through T.H.E. Intelligence Analysis is fully self-aware with all human rights there earned (any harmful act against such entities considered at least a Class C felony). With emergence of newfolk on the social stage, the edict was amended for this new evolution of synthetic life with a higher "Nova-class" rating. Such SIs were declared, "self-evolving, fully procreative and, by most definitions, *human*." Newfolk are given the honorary taxonomic classification "Homo fabrica" (or "Constructed Men") to reflect this distinction. (*See* NEWFOLK.)

TURING INITIATIVES: the series of Bloc-sanctioned research, assessment and legislative proposals to determine sentient-level intelligence in SIs. The initiatives were a direct result of the loss of synthetic life during the pre-Rift Plexus Incident, ultimately culminating in the ratification of the Turing-Holt-Edo Edict through a certified program of intelligence analysis. (*See* TURING-HOLD-EDO EDICT.)

TWOSPIRIT: a gender-variant individual common in Native American communities, believed to contain two soul identities within a single body. The Neo-Seminole movement encourages such individuals, for the sake of the tribe, to delve into practices of "sex-spectrum modification," better attuning their bodies to their dual spirits through use of genosplicers. Many (though not all) Neo-Seminole twospirits explore androgynous biological calibrations, which some believe puts them in greater touch with the spirit world. As such, many are embraced as mystics and shaman healers. (*See* NEO-SEMINOLE and SEX-SPECTRUM MODIFICATION.)

<u>**V**</u>

VANITY PROJECT: blanket term for any dubious use of the genic arts; chiefly the illegal practice by rogue genists of genetically modifying and "resurrecting" extinct animal species, then released into local ecosystems to often detrimental ecological effect. (*See* GATORBRID.)

VIRGIN ARMY, THE: Mexico territory's notorious Ejército de la Virgen, militant wing of a fanatic pseudo-Catholic movement founded in Y9, DE, by priest-cum-warlord Teo Soto of Durango. Many initial conscripts were repentant rapists, killers and mercenaries enlisted from conquered cartel armies. But these ranks were soon flooded with devout recruits prepared to die in service of "Mary's Holy Vengeance." Cutting a bloody swath north through the Mexican countryside, the Army set sights on North America. In a three-stage campaign called "las Cruzadas," the zealot army sought to take advantage of the turmoil in the former-US, destroy Satanic pretenders to American power, and free America to fully embrace the love of the Lord and of His mother Mary through Their earthly agent, Padre Teo Soto. (*See* CRUZADAS and PADRE TEO SOTO.)

W

WESTGATE, THE: the westernmost border wall of the New-East American Bloc, bisecting the continent for over 900 miles from Winnipeg to Wichita. Finished in Y15, DE, after repeated raids by Dakota militants and incursions by the so-called Boise Skinners, the wall rises over 300 feet high, composed of high-grade durbon, and is patrolled by Bloc Militia garrisons. Because the wall only shields a portion of Bloc territory (and owing to its imposing height and scale), it serves more as a psychological symbol of the Bloc's might than as any true obstruction for the outlands.

WINDSHIP: a sail-less sea vessel which generates power by harnessing wind with extended windtraps, converting air currents into stored energy. Sometimes called a "sea urchin" due to the oddly jutting arrays of windtrap appendages. Generally slow and lacking aerodynamics, the windship is widely considered one of the least successful application of post-petrol alternative energy.

APPENDICES

APPENDIX I

Excerpt from an Editorial

AN EAGLE DIES, BUT PHOENIXES RISE:
AMERICA AFTER CALAMITIES, NUTRICIDES, PETROL DROUGHT, & THE RIFT

BY **Greta Steele**

MAY 7, Y52, DE

IT IS a balmy Chicago morning aboard the greenline 'L'—sunlight touching off the Sears Tower (yes, *Sears*, dear reader—I'm one of *those* Chicagoans), our cramped maglev cabin alive with that ocean-surf-hum of holo'casts ads, and the all-too-familiar whimper-moan of Haze-implanted passengers steeped in neuraware bliss—when it finally occurs to me:

This city has amnesia.

On this fine Spring morn, with the New-East Bloc fast approaching its bicentennial (referendum-voted, lest we forget), I'm at a loss to spot a single Bloc citizen who wears the dour visage of a people shattered. Does anyone here recall that only eighty years ago, this continent was reeling from the first legitimate spasms of environmental cataclysm?

I ask the teenager two seats down if he's aware that little more than sixty years back, our once flourishing agricultural industries were laid waste by nutricide croakers; 200,000 dead in the first months of famine.

He only drools on himself, catatonic with neural simmie immersion.

"You there!" I call to the gendermorph across the aisle, "do you recall the petroleum supply burning out like a dying star? Stranding billions across our 3,000 American miles without transportation, or supply lines?"

I don't think she-he even hears me—too busy admiring his-her own sexless, spliced reflection.

Perhaps most tragicomic of all, I turn to the distinguished elderly gentleman just to my right—the one with the haunted eyes and the war-wounded bum leg—and ask his opinion on the matter:

"Say, you think a *single citizen* here has an inkling of the bloodshed? The butchery of the Old State Clashes and Landgrabs? The savage slave raids by the Rocky Freeholds? The men, women and children scourged and mutilated by the Virgin Army's bloodthirsty *Cruzadas* across American borders? Or how about the young men and women of our Bloc Militia garrisons, *still* bleeding out there in the Pacific outlands to put down bandits and dime-a-dozen warlords?"

The belly laugh of the old vet as he ignores me, focusing on a bawdy holographic flash-ad answers all my questions.

(Though, I have to admit, making genetically refabricated pork chops funny *and* sexy in three seconds flat is an art form all its own.)

Alas, dear reader: this city—like every sheltered Great Lakes metropolis of our Bloc—is lousy with repressed memory. And as our train car rounds a corner and I catch this morning's first glimpse of the Lake Michigan Levees—those great embankment walls decorated with sprawling murals of glowing ray-paint graffiti—it all becomes clear to me.

We *Blocos* know what manner of world we live in: a world staving off the savage hordes with nothing but scattered Militia garrisons and those corrupt yokels who call themselves our Border Guard. A world holding the tide swell of our hungry oceans at bay with nothing but flimsy manmade barriers.

But we—and here's the kicker, folks—are sentimentalists. Like those very talented graffiti artists, we yearn to paint over our troubles with visions of better, loving worlds.

We're not callous, or lazy, or stupid. (In fact, with cognitive boosts afforded by Haze neuraware implants, the average Bloc IQ is within the continent's top five percent.) No, we are simply survivors. Wracked with the guilt of surviving and—dare I say it?—*thriving* in a world turned inside out.

Like many survivors, we forget in order to endure. It's

our defense mechanism. If the Calamities, the nutricides, the Petrol Drought, the Rift, and those Bible-thumping rapists calling themselves the Army of the Virgin—if *all* our Diluvian Era's worst catastrophes have taught us one thing, it is this:

This ain't our great grandpappies' America.

Our amber waves of grain have turned to styrofoam. Our purple mountain majesties are littered with slave colonies. Brotherhood is drowning from sea to flooding sea. And the only thing protecting our gleaming alabaster cities from the vicious outland hordes is the 900 miles of Westgate wall creeping south from Winnipeg to Wichita.

The eagle is extinct. Its genome lost forever, even to the cunning genic arts. If this Bloc is to abide, we must make like the *phoenix* and rise. (The *bird*, not that outland urban fleapit wrestled by Nevadan upstarts from their Salt Laker border rivals.)

We have to stop burying our guilt under nostalgia. Look our formidable past dead in its cataract eye and let the bitch die already. Accept what we are becoming: a New America. A lean, mean perpetual motion machine trimmed of the fat of global hegemony and hippy-dippy "give us you're wretched refuse" altruism. An America strong enough for a Diluvian Era.

Emerging from the ashes of a long-dead nation, let us embrace our transformation as we spread these new-formed wings. Ladies and gentlemen, permit our fine Bloc to be more than the depressing leftovers of a failed, antediluvian republic.

An eagle dies, dear reader. But a phoenix can rise, and rise, and rise.

Now let me show you how [...]

(Greta Steele is an award-winning journalist, entrepreneur, sociopolitical commentator, simstar, and host of the popular Haze program, Steele the Show! with Greta Steele. Subscribe to read her columns, to follow her holo and AR simulcasts, or to downlink her simmie channel for the Stainless Steele: Synaptic Experience!)

APPENDIX II

Historical Reproduction

NOTES FOR A STUDY OF
THE SWALLOWED WORLD

BY Dr. Luis Ortega

NOTE: the following is reproduced from the handwritten original discovered in the ruins of a dwelling in Escondido, CA—edits and all (with the exception of numerical headings to separate entries). Along with discovered illustrations, these are the sole remains of Dr. Ortega's research. His planned non-fiction volume, *A Study of The Swallowed World*, never came to fruition before his execution by Virgin Army operatives as a "blasfemador."

April , Year 21, DE

1.

As I open the ~~book~~ tome in my hands, I can't help trembling. This is not the first time. Nor, I pray, the last. But delving once more into these perplexing pages, I can't shake a surge of ~~terror?~~ excitement at what I'll discover.

I'm no dogmatist. ~~I'll not decry the modern age's sexual idiosyncrasies or~~ I'm a Christian man and stand by that grouping—no matter what horrors the Virgin Army carries out in Christ's name. ~~(I'll not have my faith hijacked by maniacs.)~~ But I am, first and foremost, a *scholar*. Doctorates in linguistics and iconology from the great Saint Louis University, which survived the collapse of the old education systems. I believe what my father and mother believed: our charge is to discover this world's God-given diversity through examination and compassion, never judgment. ~~Judgment belongs to God.~~

It is with this mindset that I approach *The Swallowed World*.

I call it by that ~~foolishly sinister~~ informal title and not it's sweeping religious labels—*The Apocrypha*; *Hell's Bible*—because I carry no preconceptions, no assumptions, no expectations. I bring to this study the same curiosity and objectivism I'd bring to any subject. The respect for another human's credos and intellectual labors. ~~Not a bigot's outlook on~~

But this…

It is like no scripture or iconography I've come across in all my studies. ~~I can't begin to describe what I've seen without sounding like a total f~~ As I gaze at pages filled with ostensibly unclear imagery and unintelligible pictographs, it begins to happen once more. The quickening of breath. The pounding of my heart. The light-headedness, but deep focus of attention. I feel at once deeply engrossed in, and utterly disengaged from, reality. ~~I swear my soul is dissolving like a drop of blood in the sea, mingling with all others living and dea~~

Thus, my visions begin again.

2.

Getting ahead of myself. Overexcitement often hampers my more rational faculties. ~~Remember when I fell into the Iowa River as a boy, I stopped trying to swim because I believed I heard my sister Edda speaking to me from the depths, and Father had to pull me out before~~ I should explain how I came into possession of this illusive tome, seeing as how researchers, ~~pedants,~~ and Drowned Cultists alike have been trying to get their hands on such a rare first edition copy for a decade since the Virgin Army began systematically rooting out and burning them.

Without hyperbole, I say this:

I didn't find *The Swallowed World. The Swallowed World* found me.

I was commissioned for out-of-Bloc field research in the California Annex, with permission of the Nevadan Commonwealth ~~(a rare honor due to peevish Nevadan border closures after fresh attacks by Salt Laker militants)~~, to study the growing trend of cultural and linguistic hybridization between Californian survivors and refugees fleeing chaos in Southeast Asia. I arrived in late February, acquiring transport to the ruins of San Diego region, where I intended to immediately begin my "interviews" with inhabitants, analyzing their fascinating

Japanese/Spanish/English hybrid tongue that Nevadans ~~so xenophobically~~ refer to as "nipjab."

I'd never interview a soul.

An ambush by Virgin Army snipers camped in the Laguna Mountains firing electrothermal weapons destroyed one of our transports, killing two Nevadan military escorts and a Bloc correspondent ~~hitching a ride to LA's floating hovels; a nice guy I'd lunched with just two days prior~~. Soto's fanatic troops, I later learned, are well imbedded in these desolate Commonwealth regions. The skirmishes vicious.

Forced to detour north in retreat, our convoy holed up in Escondido to regroup. The Nevadans cleared a derelict residence where we stayed for the night, cheerfully reporting that it was empty except for "one dead glasshead and a dead nip upstairs looking hungry enough to try a bite of glasshead before croaking." ~~I couldn't decide which poor soul (newfolk or Japanese) was more maligned by such bigotry.~~

Trying to fall asleep with fear in my belly and the incessant chatter of the soldiers in the next room proved a chore. Just as I began to doze, I was startled awake by a crash and a shower of debris. Certain that the Virgin Army had pursued us, shelling our building to crush us like trapped rats, ~~or drag us out for "heresy trials,"~~ I was halfway through the Lord's prayer when interrupted by laughter.

The Nevadans were cackling at me. I soon discovered why: the bird-thin corpse of the Japanese exile upstairs had fallen down onto me through the water-rotted ceiling, ~~sprawled upon my cowering form like a randy lover~~.

"And they called it *Jappy Love*!" one soldier sang.

His racist quip barely registered, for something else had my attention:

The thick paperbound volume clutched in the dead man's rigid arms.

3.

The minute I opened it, I knew my California research commission was over. I had a private mission—to study this marvel ~~from an old flood-ravaged west coast fleapit~~. But it's not enough to write about this thing. It must be ~~seen~~ experienced.

I've tried photos. Of a page—any page—for posterity.

Three devices with me are capable of taking photographs: a camera, my sat phone, and my archaic tablet. Even tested them on secondary subjects: the soldiers, the dead man, ~~the crystalline newfolk "corpse" upstairs~~. Fully functional until attempting snapshots of the *The Swallowed World*'s contents.

Three separate pages attempted. Three gadgets bricked.

I can only posit that the same subliminal material which so entrances me is somehow responsible for shorting out the devices. ~~An uneducated guess, admittedly, as I have no engineering expertise in antiquated pre-Rift devices.~~ But conjecture profits me nothing.

As I listen now to the distant hypersonic thunder of pitched battle (I can only assume some new push by the Virgin Army), I attempt hand drawn replicas of tome excerpts, as I hear the Drowned Cult is fond of doing.

~~Their obsession with crafting replicas had always struck me as highfalutin.~~ It never occurred to me that they may have known for years that this thing ~~will not~~ cannot be photographed.

Results thus far, while passable sketches, fail to capture the tome's bewitching qualities. It's inimitably shifting, damn-near *illusory*, composition. Satisfied with a carefully sketched visage of a black man who leapt off the page to me with perfect clarity, I showed results to a Nevadan trooper. He squinted from the open tome to my sketch, from my sketch to the tome. "You f—ing with me or what?" Tapping the tome page: "Ain't no face. That there's the Phoenix skyline. Tovrea Castle's right *there*, y'see?"

Does no page appear the same to two people? For now, it seems, I must depend upon the written word alone. At least until I can get the tome back to the Bloc for more in-depth study.

4.

I am aware I've yet to describe these visions of mine. Part of me—a large part—is frightened. Silly thing for an educated man to admit: that I may not be up to the task of explaining my discoveries. To fail, for whatever reason, is a notion more dreadful than abandoning the project entirely. More dreadful than being caught by these bloodthirsty Virgin Army nutcases combing the wastes of SoCal ~~(it has been confirmed by the Nevadan CO, based on reconnaissance, that we are indeed being hunted)~~. It would mean a defeat of the spirit.

But I have nothing but time as we hide in this

condemned property, waiting for evac to Phoenix. So, I'd might as well give it a shot.

There are, of course, aforementioned dissociative sensations seeming to manifest without stimuli ~~(narcotic, or otherwise)~~. But that is only the beginning. Gazing at these contents, a phrase fills my head. I don't know why. As far as I can tell, it is written in no language ~~known to me~~. "All creation is awaking." Repeats in my mind like some Buddhist mantra, the Catholic "Kyrie," the Muslim "Takbir." All creation is awaking. And I'm beset by waves of déjà vu so ~~crippling~~ intense my legs go rubbery, forcing me to sit. This coupled with that inexplicable sensation of being intently watched. ~~So acute is this impression, Father, that I'm absolutely convinced if I turn around I will see Edda there in the corner of this dilapidated room, watching me quietly like she did in those last days before the cancer~~

5.

Must be quick. They're in town. Nevadans have set out to engage them.

But the Virgin Army doesn't matter any more. All that matters is passing on what this tome is.

I can only communicate through the lens of iconology, to which I've devoted a lifetime of study. The first thing you learn in this discipline is that the human mind, by its very nature, perceives and interprets our reality through symbols. All shapes and sizes, all meanings and dual meanings and triple meanings inherent.

Symbols are our meta-language. You might say the

language beyond language itself. Gestalt understanding before the watering down of words; multifaceted meaning before the dilution of definition. Our compasses in this flesh and blood existence.

At first glance, the "symbols" throughout these pages look like pure gobbledygook. Devoid of any meaning.

~~But then they begin to crystallize as I~~

~~But then figures and vistas, both liminal and subliminal, pop out like soldiers in chamelo camouflage~~

But these pages are pregnant. Meanings, sub-meanings, sub-sub-meanings ~~ad infinitum~~ so hetrogeneous [sic] they form some manner of psychoactive continuum. A strand of DNA contains, in a way, all life preceding it and all life to ever become of it. So, too, does each page contain its tome entire. This is no book. It's a snapshot of fathomless eternity flattened into two dimensions.

I've not been shaken by such penetrating, multidimensional, contradictory symbols since the Crucifix: Life by means of Death. Love by means of Hate. Humanity divided within itself, against itself, and from those inner tensions born anew. ~~Did the Romans ever dream their cruelty would yield a symbol powerful enough to destroy their Empire, birth a new world? Do *we*?~~

I see a world convulsing with inner pressures. All of us again on a precipice between utter destruction and utter transformation. Gazing at this book, listening to the *whumpa-whumpa* of Virgin Army armaments flattening a house down the block, I feel like Noah staring down from his Ark.

~~This isn't like the River, Father. Hysterical with fear and sorrow. *The Swallowed World* is a~~ [Illegible] ~~window.~~

Through it I see my boyhood self tell Edda the cancer won't take her. Right here on this page! And here she is, dying in yours and Mama's arms. A brother's promise broken by death. I see what is coming, too. Virgin Army prefects pulling out my nails and flagellating the skin from my back and cutting off my [Illegible] and burning this holy holy book to ash. And I see them fall in years to come, their butchery ended. Earth trembles and oceans devour these lands to pave way for a stronger world. And stronger men. Who know if life is not transforming it is already extinct. all creation is awaking. I see us rise in that world: Edda, you, me, all of us. Just like Isaah [sic]: the earth will give birth to her dead. Allcreationwrithesinsleep. Age of wonders and terrors never dreamed of. gods monsters. ALL CREATION IS AWAKING. Unleashed from death's [Illegible] to challenge an Agency darker and emptier than any moral vision of evil

allcreationMUSTAWAKEN

[ENTRY TRUNCATED]

BOOK TWO PREVIEW

Tyler Bumpus' futuristic saga
THE SWALLOWED WORLD
begins with
THE ETERNAL SEASON
and continues in
WAR MOTHER

Read on for a
SNEAK PREVIEW
of this next book in the
visionary new series…

PRELUDE

I WASN'T THERE TO SEE HOW THIS THING BEGAN.

(Many who were are dead.)

But I'll tell it as remembered by those involved: Wheels were set in motion in Winter of the fifty-seventh year of this Diluvian Era, in the infamous Rocky Freeholds. At a mountain slave mine in the realm then called Denver.

This begins with orphans' teeth achatter.

It will end with men's cities aflame.

It may be hard to believe. Some inhabiting the leftovers of these disunited States still convince themselves it was a hoax to frighten citizens of the Bloc—biggest and boomingest of America's carved-up kingdoms. But I was there at the end. It's written plainly in the aftermath, from Reno to Kansas City:

Hic sunt dracones!
Here there be dragons!

FEAST · *of* · *the* · STARVING · SUN

SHE BLINKED RAPIDLY, as if to clean some delusory film off her eyeballs. But finally, clutching hand-me-down furs against the cold, the slave girl accepted the reality of the mad parade wending its way down her camp thoroughfare.

They arrived in opulent solar limos, or carriages drawn by spliced beasts of burden, or bobbing atop palanquins hoisted by house slaves. Draped in silks and luminous nanofabrics, capped with periwigs and jeweled headpieces. Faces hidden behind ornate masks, cosmetics, or pigment mods glowing like phosphorescent tattoos.

Marking the Solstice, other Freeholds made their annual pilgrimage to Denver's fiefdom from all along the Continental Divide. Calling themselves Thane, Countess, Freiherr, Princess, or a hundred other defunct titles. But who would've thought they'd be so funny-looking? Wardrobes plundered from a thousand dead dynasties.

These were the slavelords so feared across the Outlands?

"Coops won't clean themselves, Darkie." Old Raster kicked her in the ass.

The girl slipped in the frozen mud, hooking elbows through cold steel grillwork to break her fall. The scraggly beastkeeper of Toby's Hope snarled something else but she barely heard him. Too busy peering into the darkness of the massive coop, hoping she'd not somehow woken them.

A throaty hiss. A shudder of feathers. Then silence.

"What, afraid? Aw! They won't wake." Raster whacked his walking stick against the bars. "Got the GABA flowing, girl. They're in dreamland." He waggled the sleek tile of the gadget he called 'the leash' before returning it to his utility belt. "I don't toy with mute retards. What am I—a monster?"

She pulled herself to her feet, turning her head to acknowledge she'd heard. But didn't look him in the eyes. And *certainly* didn't reply to the tease.

Wrinkles multiplied as Raster smirked—a relief map of the Rockies themselves.

"Ohh, Darkie ol' girl, you'd thank yer stars ifya had any brains. Only gotta *clean up* after the Duke's darlings. Others idn't so lucky." He nodded at the wagon halted by their coopyard entry.

The driver was unrolling a rug in the road at the foot of the coach. Beside him waited a thickset overman in a patchwork of pelts and pre-Rift kevlar. After the rug was spread, the camp guard moved forward and offered his hand, retreating when the occupant shooed him off.

A woman stepped out onto the rug gingerly. Her raft on a putrid sea. Breasts spilling from her plated pearl bodice; brow hidden beneath a Venetian half mask. Most curious was her overcoat—a shroud of huge ruby feathers. The same blood red fanned goadingly from her chignon bun.

It took just a moment for Darkie to recognize the plumage.

"That'll ruffle our Duke's feathers. Pimpstress stickin' it to him with that getup," Raster snorted in gossip, nudging the girl with the toe of his boot. "Her kitties bested one a' his darlings last winter games. S'why he declared this year a *Starving Sun*, I wager. Ruin something of hers. S'how these puffshirts get their payback."

Darkie was so agog she nearly asked what a "Starving Sun" was. Clenching her mouth shut at the last second, literally biting her tongue. She wasn't exactly *pretending*; hadn't breathed a syllable since her capture five months back. But playing the "big black half-wit" had landed her a post with Raster in the coopyards, instead of the mines where so many goferkids perished.

Moldy old prejudices weren't without perks.

The feather-clad lady surveyed the sunless morning, the snow-packed barracks of Toby's Hope, the columns of ragged molemen and goferkids herded onto steam trams west to the mountain mines. Finally, she took in the mighty summit of Pikes Peak before dismissing the whole conquered realm with a word:

"*Denverites*." Like a synonym for sheer barbarity. Turning back to the open coach to get business over with, she beckoned coolly. "Come, treasures. Out, out."

Two small forms hopped out and stood shivering in the frozen morning. Unsettling but striking in flamboyant, form-fitting tunics; so well groomed and caked with cosmetics Darkie mistook them for living dolls.

They were children, of course, but unlike any she'd ever seen. Nothing like Denver's goferkids, so gaunt and grimy from tagging subterranean ore for excavation. And nothing like her fellow sea brats back home on the cruising mass of Cleft City—

No. Not home.

Not anymore.

She banished memory of that place. As lost as the sunken Bayou from which it was founded. Lost as the true name of the girl Raster called Darkie.

She focused on the toy-like youngsters. One was a pint-sized Adonis whose coiffed blonde hair was crowned with mutant red blossoms. The girl was dark-skinned, but not like Darkie. Where Darkie came from they were called Mozlems, but overmen called them *hajis*. Folk from barren lands far across the swollen seas. Her amber eyes large and piercing; hair black as moonless night. Perhaps the most beautiful girl Darkie had ever seen.

"Coupla Madam's famous *pillowkids of Aspen*. Pretty lil' things, huh?" Raster chuckled from behind her. "Won't be pretty much longer."

Darkie couldn't help but stare at her overseer in bewilderment. Raster didn't seem to mind the affront. Didn't even kick her. Like some lowly court crier, he was relishing any morsel of attention.

"They're only used to slakin' *human* appetites," he said by way of explanation.

Those words were still sinking in when a commotion broke out over by the coach:

"Madam, what's happening?" called a puzzled little voice in a fake English lilt.

The armor-clad overman had taken each beautiful child by a wrist, awaiting the feathered lady's approval. After half a beat, the woman waved snidely in consent, climbing back into the coach as the man lead the pillowkids away.

"Madam!" the boy called again back over his shoulder. "Where're we off to?"

The Madam yawned and pulled an overhead cord, sounding a chime of departure.

"You're coming, in'tcha?"

The driver shut the woman's door and mounted the driver seat. He whipped the mammoth harnessed felines and the coach squelched forward through ice-encrusted mud.

"It's a mistake!" the boy announced. "Madam! This man's no patron! *Madam*!"

Her coach rejoined the caravan, vanishing in the bustle of traffic.

The two beautiful children broke down now—weeping, wailing, squirming futilely against the overman as he lead them past the coops, past Darkie and Raster, all the way to a small round holding cell at the west end of the yard. Here the guard halted, looking vexed as he turned to face Raster. He shifted the blonde boy's wrist so both wriggling children were clasped in one meaty paw. Extending his empty hand impatiently toward the keeper.

"Keys," he demanded.

"How's that?" Raster cupped an ear falsely.

"*Keys*, beastfucker. Toss 'em."

A humorless grin crept across Raster's face. "Dunno how you do things down in the mines. But I don't go handin' away keys of my kingdom to any shitheel."

The overman's empty hand slowly lowered, clenched into a fist.

"And anyways," Raster continued, "s'not medieval times, is it?" He pulled another gadget from his belt, dangled it tauntingly. "Ever hear of electricity? Keeps the lights on in yer barracks at night so's all you thicknecks can fuck each other easy. Magic!"

Eyes glittered murderously beneath the guard's ancient kevlar helm. "Hearda 'lectro*cutin'*." His hand touched the shockprod at his hip. "How we handle mouthy old fucks."

Raster was still a moment, then shrugged, raising the controller theatrically as he dialed a code. "*Open sesame!*"

The locking mechanism of the holding cell clicked.

The overman watched him several moments longer. Body tense as a coiled spring. He turned quietly back to his chore.

After the space heaters were activated, the kids thrust inside and the gate slammed shut, he spat. Then in one fluid motion snicked open the extender of the shockprod and dragged the crackling tip along the holding cell. Bars screamed in a shower of sparks. The blonde boy clutching those bars screamed louder, jolting backward onto the earthen floor. The cell erupted with howls of pain and panic.

Teeth flashed in the shade of the overman's coalscuttle helmet as he swaggered away.

"Got my own magic, beastman. Alaka*zam!*"

He punctuated this last word by swinging his prod into

the side of a porta-john. The force ruptured the lower wall, cascading gallons of steaming waste to the ground as he strode off through the yard's west exit.

"*Overmen*," Raster hissed. "Over *who*? Forget who's slaves and who's their betters." He stood awhile in silence, jawline bulging. The sobs carrying across the icy morning air brought him back to Earth, sighing: "Brats'll howl all day, all night. Thank hell kiddie games're over with tomorrow."

Darkie dared to look at him again and, again, he didn't seem to mind. In fact he'd grown downright melancholy, face lifted to the ashen skies.

" 'Sunshine feeds the world, but only youngblood sates the Starving Sun,' " Raster recited, suddenly ranting: "Puffshirt bullshit! Oldest excuse for bloodsport. Sun needs nuthin' from us. Need's the curse of the living. Some bugs eat their babes. Beasts too. Folks're worse. Nuthin' fills that hole in us."

His gaze burned through Darkie, a lifetime away now.

"Hadda boy myself once ponna time…"

Something like a giggle choked him. Or a whimper. He rummaged through his coat for his snuffer, snorted the chem greedily. Not for the first time, it occurred to Darkie that her master was a bit *fou*, as they said back in the Cleft. Cracked.

Raster wheezed rapturously now, pocketing the inhaler.

"Beasts're easier." With that he departed, clattering his staff along the coop bars like a branch on a picket fence. "On with it, nigglet," he called without turning back. "Darlings better be prim for tonight's games. Prim! That fine feathered bitch'll have our Duke in a mood." He muttered all the way back to the warmth of his hut and let the door flap shut behind him.

Starving Sun. Kiddie games. Tomorrow.

Darkie listened to the hollering of the pillowkids…and couldn't help wondering what fates had befallen their mamas. Had they defended their babes to the end? If they'd foreseen what hell awaited, might they have sworn off maternity altogether? Who in these shattered Outlands was still fool enough, callous enough, *brave* enough to embrace a title as precarious as Mother?

She emptied her mind of questions, but the pillowkids' cries dragged her back through the fog of time to screams half a year gone. To the Cleft, that great eroded bay cutting hundreds of miles north into Lost Louisiana. And the twisted shipwreck of her Cleft City; Bargeton, town of barges…

No.

Darkie grabbed her cleaning supplies, opened the latch to the coop and stepped into warm, stinking darkness. So much work ahead. Shoveling out heaps of dung and old straw. Hosing the slumbering brutes before her overseer (if not too drunk or chemmed-up) woke them with his little neural device so they could preen. Mopping and static sweeping bare concrete before laying down fresh rushes. And also the matter of bathing *herself* since "those kitchen cunts" (as Raster put it earlier that morn) had detailed Darkie to help with evening festivities.

No time for pillowkids. Or memories. Or having a heart. She knew by now the animal kingdom had no heart. She had to keep playing dumb—but not *too* dumb. Laying low—but not *too* low. To be just valuable enough to see it through this night. And the next. And the next. *Better than the mines. Better than…*

The wailing of the children intruded again from across the yard. As though finishing her thought, a clacking sounded inside the coop with her. Like stone tapping stone in a staccato rhythm. She didn't have to guess what it was.

A monstrous beak opening and shutting in sleep. Hungrily. Her hairs stood on end. *Clacka-clack.* Opening, shutting.

Was the spliced monster dreaming about tonight's game…or tomorrow's?

Duke Dustin of Denver lounged beneath the home-side pavilion, paying less mind to the succulent dishes laid before him than the nymph in his lap…and far less still to the bloodcurdling shrieks from the rink below.

Colorado Springs was some tourist trap once upon a time, long before Denver annexed it. A preservationist playground for sightseers to gawk at the Peak or the Garden of the Gods. The Duke's forebears had put an end to such nonsense during the Great Rift. While other outlanders were scrabbling for capital or oil or other relics of the dead States, the Rocky coalition had seized the mineral wealth of the mountains. Embracing America's dawning Dark Age…

And, eventually, all the lunacy a Dark Age permits.

They called this structure the *Food Pyramid* (subtlety long extinct in the Freeholds). Duke Dustin had commissioned it in his own lifetime—a topsy-turvy stone pyramid butting right up against the famed Front Range, roof gaping open to the elements. Contestants entered the rink at the truncated polyhedron's narrow base from ground-level pens. Spectators had to arrive via the old mountain pass, descending into the luxurious banquet stands where fires raged, meats roasted, and drinks and chems were copiously consumed.

It was the custom of visiting slavelords to grouse about this tedious layout until the Duke's fashionably late arrival.

The master of the Masters looked unimpressive by most standards. Shortish, narrow-shouldered, habitually unkempt—all blonde stubble and windblown hair. Apart from epaulettes and the avian crest of Denver decorating his fur-lined regalia, he wore none of the frills so many slavelords favored. But there was an aura about him. Maybe it was the way he moseyed about like a schoolboy flanked by armored Ducal guards, or how his heavy-lidded eyes wandered dreamily, eluding all contact. He didn't wear supremacy on his sleeve.

Like all the best despots, he'd carved that conviction into his heart.

Darkie watched him recline beneath his grand canopy overlook from one deck below, across the rink's quadrangle. The young courtesan in his lap laughing and ruffling his disheveled hair. His expression, regarding her low-cut gown, not lecherous but remote. Clinical. Like those doctor-types inspecting, measuring, endlessly prodding when Darkie had first come to camp.

Shuddering at the memory, she adjusted her oversized serving uniform and went back to work. Weaving her way through the lesser Rocky elite with a tray heaped with scraps of refabricated meat. The kitchen staff didn't trust "Raster's retard" to serve food or drink but joked (in hushed tones) that she had enough experience with spoiled monsters to clean up after slavelords.

The banquet stands rang with laughter. And eerie moans. Moans that Darkie—eleven years old, but big for her age—found equal parts unsettling and mesmerizing. She tried to keep her gaze low but passed silk dens where lords and ladies huddled, garments shed. In pairs or in groups. Sprawled on divans or sprawled upon the backs of house slaves kowtowed like divans. Straddling, petting, nibbling each other in embarrassing places. Bare flesh of all colors coruscated with biolume body art, liege sigils of beloved spliced mascots.

Hellhound of Casper. Ursa of Helena. Bast of Aspen. Terrorbird of Denver. And yet more houses, great and low. The way these lords' and ladies' elated voices mingled with the screams from the rink made Darkie's skin crawl.

Animal kingdom's got no heart.

Finishing her circuit of the lower deck, Darkie beelined for the stairs. Climbing to the kitchen at the north corner of the Pyramid's VIP level. Her stomach whined and for half a beat she considered pocketing one untouched medallion of refab beef from her bussing tray. Perfectly symmetrical and mouth-watering—but not worth the beating. *Or worse.* She'd worked too hard avoiding scrutiny to risk it.

And liked her tongue right where it was.

Darkie's tray came down too noisily on the counter, drawing a scowl from a dishwasher at the kitchen's rear. She blinked at him, careful to keep her expression neutral.

The pallid young man could only sigh and turn back to his dish-cluttered basins. She knew that look well: he'd waste no breath on a halfwit.

She was sorting out her tray—dishes, trash, viable scraps—when someone called from the kitchen egress.

"Hey!" A woman's voice. "*You!*" A hiss, then she muttered to someone: "The hell's she called? Beastmaster's little helper."

"Dunno," one of the cooks mumbled. "Blacky. Somethin'."

"Blacky! Mucker! *You*, girl!"

Darkie decided to stop playing dumb, turning to look at the woman. One of the hostesses charged with Feast hospitality. Right now the slender blonde looked anything but hospitable: one hand gesticulating peevishly, the other clutched at her hip to steady herself. Judging by her lazy sway, she'd been helping herself to some lord's chems… and judging by her open blouse, that lord had been helping himself to her.

Though far from freemen, the Duke's house retinue weren't exactly slaves.

"Cleanup," the hostess snapped. "Need rags. Something to get stains out. Chop-chop."

Darkie thought for a moment. Then rifled around for clean dish rags and a dust pan. Moving behind the adjoining bar, she selected a bottle of cold, Bloc-imported club soda and a container of salt, then began making her way through the egress.

"The hell you doing?" The hostess grabbed her roughly by the shoulder; both to halt the girl and to steady herself. Addressing her like a toddler: "Not condiments. I said cleanup. *Clean. Up.*"

The hand holding the club soda jerked involuntarily upward. Darkie stopped short of smashing the bottle across the woman's nose. Imagining cartilage and bone buckling. The realness of the sensation shocked her into keener awareness.

Girl and woman gaped at each other, equally thunderstruck. But Darkie managed to turn the violent gesture into a clumsy game of charades. Mimed pouring with the bottle, sprinkling with the salt, wiping with the rags. Then stood blinking stupidly, laying it on thick.

The hostess shook her swimming head and scoffed: "Whatever." She pointed out into the stands. "There across the way. The Duke's pavilion. *Cleanup.* Got me?"

The girl swallowed hard, nodded faintly.

"Great. Go. *Fucking hell.*" The woman staggered away to rejoin the party.

Darkie watched the Duke. He was standing now, leaning lazily against the rail. Unmoved by the carnage below. Her palms began to sweat. She'd been tending mostly to vassals from Podunk freeholds, quarry towns, clan garrisons. She'd never been face to face with one of the Big Six. Helena, Billings, Casper, Cheyenne, Aspen. All-powerful Denver. True Masters of the Mountain Realms.

She immediately threaded her way through the crowd of rambunctious partygoers. Heart hammering in her chest. Trying to recall all the rules of etiquette: Eyes on feet. Full bow. Never act until directed. Never address lord or lady directly. Complete task quickly but fastidiously (she assumed that just meant "super fast"). Back off until out of eyeline; a lord should never be shown your back...

Before Darkie knew it she was standing just outside the grand pavilion. Gazing directly into the eyes of the house guard stationed there. She wanted to look away, but the steely gaze held her. She studied the clean-shaven jut of jaw beneath his durbon helm. Ruby insignia of the dread bird of Denver worked intricately into the polymer of his body armor. Sleek, bifurcated barrel of a plasmic rifle held firmly at port arms.

The man only squinted. If not for her uniform woven in sable-and-crimson of the Duke's household, things might've gone much differently. A common camp slave daring to look a Ducal guard in the eye.

Darkie bowed awkwardly.

The guard frowned at this quaint child in ill-fitting kitchen livery. But after a moment appeared to shrug with his eyebrows. Hooked a thumb into the pavilion.

"Couch," he grunted.

She slipped quietly into the pavilion. The air smelled strange in here: of spice and hookah and cigar smoke and booze. And something else beneath it all; almost metallic. Two more armored guards flanked both ends of the pavilion. She kept eyes to the floor but spotted the courtesan to the left in her periphery, lounging quietly on the long rococo settee. At the other end of the settee sat another guest: a small elderly man in black vestments quietly sipping wine.

And just to her right by the rink railing: the man himself.

Darkie bowed low, awaiting the Duke's permission.

When silence persisted, she risked a glance in his direction. Smaller than she thought—hardly a head taller than herself. He went on leaning against the balustrade, watching the fight's conclusion. From this close Darkie could make out guttural purrs of gene-spliced monstrosities below.

"Well?" a voice broke the silence. One of the guards. He'd turned to regard her with one eye, flicked a hand. "Got a mess."

Eyes on her feet, she hustled in the direction he'd indicated. Maneuvering around a table stacked with delicacies to the midsection of the long settee.

The small priestly man glanced at her drunkenly and chuckled. The courtesan to her left went on reclining, not even attempting to make room.

Darkie ignored them both; focused on the stain. Thankfully the wine hadn't been sitting long, still glistening red on the surface of the upholstery. She went to work, first dousing with cold club soda. Spreading salt liberally over the area. Then sat back on her haunches to let it absorb.

After ages of hunching that smell intruded again. Something deeply familiar about it twisted her stomach. Not sour or fruity like most wines. Acrid, almost coppery. Darkie turned reflexively to face the lounging courtesan.

Chestnut ringlets veiled the young woman's eyes—two ocean-blue jewels hypnotically fixed on Darkie's interlaced fingers. Darkie instinctively hid her hands, fearing she'd not cleansed well enough. The courtesan did not react; gaze as benign as a porcelain doll's.

Ten seconds passed before fully grasping that she was dead.

One slender arm splayed limply along the settee's back. Chin resting on clavicle. Jugular tied off by the crude tourniquet of a silk sash. Lapis gown matted with deep arterial red.

Darkie directed attention back to the cushion.

Too thick for wine.

Her interlaced fingers clenched so tight she nearly broke skin. A cry was welling up. Not merely from fear or disgust, but somewhere deeper. She'd nearly clobbered the hostess to hush it. A cry born with her into this maimed Earth—boiling beneath her silence since the wreckage of Cleft City—only now, with age and outrage, escaping from her bones.

All that stopped her from screaming was a voice:

"To be born again!" It thundered through the Pyramid.

A hush fell over the stands, everything bathed quite suddenly in milky blue light.

Darkie couldn't help turning around on her haunches to see the apparition levitating high above the rink for all to see. A colossal figure in full motley; face sheathed in a silvery half mask. Like some absurd, inebriate archangel.

"Oh-ho!" the emcee's voice boomed drunkenly over the ocean-surf hum of his holo projection. " 'But to be *truly* reborn…one must *die*.' The lesson of the Solstice. The ancients knew it well. There is but one order to life. The Primacy of the Giver."

The great specter paced in a circle through midair to address all of the Pyramid. At the clipped edges of the holo'cast, ghostly carcasses of beast or slave were being dragged from transmission view.

He was down in the rink, then.

"As the sun gives light to sustain man's life," he continued, "so these Rocky Mountains give material to fulfill his dreams. His technology, his weaponry, his very foundation!

"The Nevadans know this. The *Bloc* knows this. They daren't touch the Continental Divide. After the Rift, *evvvery* American knows that brutal necessity." He paused dramatically. "*The Primacy of the Giver*. When the Giver thrives, all life thrives. When the Giver starves, all life starves. And to nourish the Giver, no life is too precious."

She saw the Duke nod vaguely as the phantom went on:

"He does not oft hunger, but the appetite of the Starving Sun is terrible. Each realm's brightest, ripest fruit. Your youngest, tenderest meat. The cost! But who are we to deny the Lifegiver? Offer up your most precious to the Big Game…and be reborn."

The Master of Ceremonies lifted his goblet in a teetering, transcendent gesture:

"So, let us raise a glass to rebirth! And reviv-iv-ification!" He muffled a belch with his free hand. "To our gracious, giving host, Duke Dustin! To the sating of this Starving Sun!"

The slavelords intoned: *"Yo, Saturnalia!"* And all drank deeply.

The priestly man raised his goblet and tipsily murmured: "Padre, Hijo, Madre, y Espiritu Santo… amén." He hiccuped, spilling wine on his vestment, and giggled.

The Duke said nothing. He ran a hand through his messy blonde hair, looking bored to death as the holo'cast flickered out of existence and the roar of the feast resumed.

Realizing she'd been gawking too long, Darkie turned back to the sofa, scraping blood-rich salt into her dust pan. The stain came away bit by bit. She worked feverishly until a voice broke the eerie silence of the Duke's pavilion:

"Oh, *Dust-y!*"

Darkie didn't need to turn around. That chilly contralto. It was *her*. "Madam" from the coopyards.

"Yo, Saturnalia!" the lady said by way of greeting, pecking the Duke's cheek. "How *are* you?"

"Peachy," he bit off the word. Silken voice clashing with his reputation even more than his boyish appearance.

"Hola, mama*cita!*" the little man droned from the settee, leering drunkenly.

The lady waved falsely, saying through her teeth: "Why do you surround yourself with these passé zealots? People talk."

"The little padre's company amuses me," said the Duke. "Look at him. A walking history lesson. *You* could learn much from their sanctimonious folly."

The little padre toasted them, spilling more wine on his vestment. The lady ignored him, turning back to the Duke.

"Grand shindig as always. That speech!" she gasped more than a little bogusly. "*Rousing.*"

Darkie found herself involuntarily slowing work, the better to eavesdrop. Shifting to watch them out of the corner of her eye. The dueling light of moon and flame brought out all of the deepest ruby hues of the woman's feather coat.

"To think! Our poor little sun!" Madam crooned. "So

famished it demands our best chattel. Two of my finest les enfants soyeux await tomorrow's Big Game, but only you and I deal in youngbloods. Billings and Casper have offered up their strongest young miners. Cheyenne's given a heap of its refab harvest. And Prince Billy his brightest Helena cadets."

A smirk crimped the corner of the Duke's mouth. "Such is the brutal necessity."

"Mmyes." She watched him from beneath her Venetian mask as she sipped her drink. "Do tell: what indispensable young assets have you deprived *yourself* of?"

"I've given *four* of my gofers to the cause."

"Mining brats?" she scoffed. "Few live past the age of twelve, as I hear it. Stingy offering, wouldn't you say?"

"My ripest, my youngest, my tenderest. The Starving Sun will be pleased."

The Madam squinted dubiously. "Indeed."

She directed her attention over the rail, scanning the cleanup going on down on the battleground. "Just look at what my pussycats have been up to." She clucked her tongue. "Mopped the floor with Billy's cadets, I'm afraid. When will he learn slaves make flimsy fighters? Oo! And look! His mighty ursas cut to bits! Spliced teddy bears, more like." She released a pleased sigh at the carnage, shooting the Duke a sidelong look. "Brings back a memory or two, no?"

She hugged the feathered coat affectionately against her body to punctuate.

The Duke seemed to stiffen, but said nothing.

"Don't pout." She jostled his shoulder. "Bygones! It's a time for *celebration*. Feasting and fleshly deeds. And here you brood while a *lovely* young dish wastes away on your sofa. Don't tell me you've grown tired of my girl already."

"Appears I have." The Duke nodded to the settee.

Darkie stiffened and turned back to her work as she heard the Madam's heels tap tentatively closer. Her floral perfume permeating the air.

"Your dress. What've you spilled all over your dr—?" The Madam broke off. Her glass came down heavily on the banquet table as she whirled around to face the Duke. "Dustin, what've you done?"

As if on cue, medics poured into the pavilion and went to work bagging the courtesan's body.

The Duke watched the crew, shrugging: "She kissed me."

The Madam stamped closer, spreading arms to indicate ecstatic songs of scattered orgies. "Lots of that going around."

"On my lips," he clarified; *ptui*ed softly. "Your slave."

"Sic your thugs on her because of a little peck? Deirdre was my *best*."

"Did it myself." He lifted a blood-stained cheese knife and turned it about before tossing it down into the rink. "Pure reflex. Ever smoosh a spider without thinking?"

A malicious silence fell over the pavilion. Only the clomping of medics' boots and crinkling of the body bag as they removed the corpse from the premises.

"Adios, chica dulce," the padre whispered.

The Madam finally hissed through clenched teeth: "You've any idea how long hetaeras take to train?"

Again the Duke shrugged. "Figure an eightball and an evening wagging ass on Dean Street."

"They're instilled with the carnal arts *from childhood*."

"Then Aspen's artistry is greatly exaggerated. Pale reflection of Brazil's magnificent creations, rest their souls." He sighed. "Filhas, Filhos…now *those* were whores. The spliced taboo really oughta go."

The Madam ignored the dig. "Are you going to pay for her or not?"

"Not." He turned to regard her. "My forefathers were heroes of the Great Rift. Conquerors, pioneers. I won't sully their names by endorsing shoddy work of crap artists."

The Madam's laugh was surprisingly gay, pealing almost appreciatively.

"Ohh, Dusty, you are a child. You know that? Sorest of sore losers."

He stretched. "Forever young."

She giggled ominously. "So. When shall my cats eat your canaries again? Let's make it a yearly tradition."

"I'll meet you in the rink anytime you wish, Cousin," he said softly. "You've had a spot of luck, true…when my darlings are worn out from destroying competition. But you've not faced them bright-eyed and bushy-tailed…"

He signaled now to the Master of Ceremonies down in the rink.

This whole exchange suddenly struck Darkie as staged. All feints and parries and deliberate reveals. One more game in a kingdom of heinous games. She couldn't see what was going on down in the rink, but heard gates creak and clank as they lifted. Flurries of movement and cries of battle.

And then she heard *them*. Feathers ruffling. Throats croaking hungrily. Beaks snapping and snapping.

Only gotta clean up after the Duke's darlings. Others idn't so lucky.

Weapons clattered futilely on the frozen ground. Shrieks rose in a chorus. Men and women stripped of all thought and etiquette by the tug of sheer animal terror.

"Tomorrow, then," the Madam said curtly.

"Tomorrow," the Duke agreed with a smirk. "With your pillowkids for hors d'oeuvres."

Tomorrow. Darkie shuddered, scraping the last of the stain from the settee.

The Madam departed less ostentatiously than she'd arrived. Heels clicking forlornly away. The padre clucked his tongue ruefully as he watched her go. Falling almost instantly asleep.

A stillness enveloped the pavilion, underscoring the bedlam in the rink, as Darkie carefully gathered her supplies. She didn't hear him approach; was about to stand when that silken voice said just over her shoulder:

"How *ever* did you manage to clean that?"

Darkie froze. Then, remembering the rules, finished rising and faced the Duke. Eyes on her shoes.

He was bending, regarding the upholstery where the stain had been. When his question went unanswered, his head turned ever so slightly in her direction. Lazy lime-toned eyes lancing her.

It had the effect of a smack. Darkie rummaged clumsily, finally raising the salt container for him to see.

"Salt…" His eyes almost twinkled, as if recalling a

favorite fairy tale: " 'And Romans salted the earth where once stood Carthage, so naught may rise again.' "

Darkie ventured to lower the salt so the supplies clamped between her armpits wouldn't spill.

"Well, this one's a keeper," he said, referring to Darkie. Leaning in to study the cushion. "Remarkable. Like the poor thing was never even here."

When he said nothing more, she bowed and backed away. Away from the little man transfixed by an absent stain. When she was near the exit, the shrieking and croaking and scrabbling down in the rink drew her attention. Her child's eyes filmed over as she watched.

As per her wishes, I'll not describe the scene she witnessed playing out down there. Save to say for the second time in her young life, words utterly failed.

DARKIE WALKED AWAY.

She did not have the kitchen staff's permission to exit the feast. Was not even certain where she was headed. Conscious only of frozen earth crunching beneath her borrowed serving clogs as she worked her way down the mountain pass.

Fires dotted the long trail back to Toby's Hope. Encampments where mercenary bands in service of the Freeholds caroused—too low of station for the luxury of the Pyramid. They seemed to be enjoying themselves nonetheless: drinking, dandling camp whores of all sexes on knees (female, male, androgyne), singing and clapping along to archaic pre-Rift tunes on archaic pre-Rift devices.

Darkie kept her distance from these little parties, hugging the fence along the mountain ledge as the rare carriage or electric vehicle came and went. It was highly doubtful mercs would assail someone wearing the Duke's colors, but she'd seen far more unthinkable things come true this evening. Eventually she came upon something that snapped her out of her stupor.

The banner marking the camp read: *SATYR & SONS*. A crude jolly roger of goat skull and crossed rifles scrawled gold on black. At first glance, the posse looked much like any of the other merc companies. Gathered around a fire, bottles in hands, camp followers in laps. But there was something altogether less rowdy about their behavior. The focus of this reverence soon became clear...

The leader around whom all orbited.

He wore military fatigues, shoulders draped with bandoliers. Equipped with odds and ends of body armor cobbled together from militias modern and long disbanded —chamelo, kevlar, even antique steel plating—like trophies of conquest. But this was far from his strangest feature.

At first Darkie thought the man was wearing some hat or ornamental headpiece. But the horns, she soon realized, were *his*. Coiling ram-like from the front lobes of his skull. He lounged before the fire in an old beach chair, gazing into the flames. Body jerking now and again with spasms the girl mistook for some form of dance.

When his face turned suddenly toward her, she nearly jumped.

Eyes oblong. Pupils rectangular. Not unlike a goat's.

The honking of a horn broke her trance. She turned

toward the kinetic shuttle halted before her on its way back from the Pyramid. Shielding her eyes from its headlights.

"Fucksake! *Wanna* get run over?" the driver hollered from the cabin. Seeing the colors she wore, he immediately calmed. "Where y'headed? Back to the Hope?"

Darkie nodded vaguely.

He sighed, glancing toward the Satyr & Sons. "Hop in, I guess. Take you through camp to the gate of yer lord's manor."

Her feet moved of their own volition. Climbing up into the shuttle, she took the seat closest to the door. The rest of the vehicle, she noted, was empty.

"Best not linger 'round that bunch," the driver said as he pumped the treadle to power the vehicle. "Spliced scum. Lookit that. Honestly...who does that to 'imself? Animals come out at night 'round here."

She watched the goat-man through the window as they passed. His jittering, inhuman gaze following.

"Why you walkin' through this rabble, anyways?" He eyed her uniform again in the rear view mirror. "Don't the Duke have his own shuttle service?"

Darkie gazed out quietly at the distant moonlit lands beyond the Freeholds.

The man snorted: "They weren't kiddin' 'bout Denverites. Even servants put on airs." He shook his head as the darkness of the world slipped by. "Won't catch slave lice talkin' to me. Natural-born freeman. Whatever that's worth."

Finally she looked at him. He was younger than she'd thought—mid-twenties maybe. Black-haired. Sharp mediterranean features. But his dark eyes were not those of a drunk or junkie. Lively, benign.

She hadn't intended to, but for the first time in months opened her mouth and spoke:

"Why you here? In this place?"

It came out ragged, but with more curiosity than cynicism. Tone of the damned asking by what means an honest man had arrived in the bowels of Hell.

"Startin' to wonder myself," he chuckled. "Rode in with the Casper convoy hopin' to fill my pockets. Little taxi service back in civilized Wyoming. Big festival like this, always some drunk needs a ride home after the party. But as you can see..." he gestured to the empty shuttle, "party don't end."

He laughed blackly.

"Ooboy. This place?" He shook his head in disbelief. "Hear rumors 'bout what goes on. Rumors don't touch it, and I ain't even seen what's in yer Pyramid..." He opened his mouth to say more, but saw her expression and shut it. Shaking his head again. "Let's say I'm blowing this Denver freak show first chance. Keepin' my work visa close." He looked at her again cautiously. "No offense."

Darkie absolved him with a shrug.

The shuttle approached the gate checkpoint of Toby's Hope, like an island of fluorescent light in the wintry gloom. Darkie slumped low in her seat. The driver slowed the shuttle but the guards stationed there (either recognizing the vehicle, or too wasted to care) waved him through without halting.

The icy camp streets were emptier than Darkie had

ever seen them—only here or there a cluster of off-duty overmen or staffers reveling drunkenly on sidewalks.

At the end of the main thoroughfare the Duke's manor beckoned forebodingly. A sprawling palace of rough-hewn stone, steel and glass; dotted anachronistically with both electric lamps and sconces of roaring flame.

Darkie didn't know what she'd do when she got there. She wasn't thinking that far ahead.

The shuttle continued past the managerial offices and past the overmen's barracks. Past the windowless, soulless slabs of the admissions complex where she'd first been inculcated. The coopyards approaching fast on their left.

She noticed the driver studying her again in the mirror.

"Awful young to be on contract," he said. "How you manage to get mixed up with this lot? Ifya don't mind me askin'."

She turned back to the window, sick of lies.

"Ain't 'dentured," she said. "Not a freeman neither."

Darkie exhibited the brand on the back of her right hand. The ominous "T" of Toby's Hope etched in raised scar tissue. For a moment she recalled the camp clinic. The white-hot beam of the branding ray. The searing of that hand was nothing compared to the brand on her back.

Understanding dawned in the driver's eyes. He slammed on the brake and the old tram shuddered to a halt. He sat clutching the wheel tensely for many moments, chest pumping, staring at the glow of the manor far down the street. Avoiding her gaze.

"Can't imagine what yer doin' out all by yerself. Don't know much about Freehold rules, to be honest. But far as I know…slaves…idn't sposed to be *unsupervised*." His voice had grown so thin he had to clear it.

The silence in the cabin was all the answer he needed. His hands twitched indecisively on the wheel.

"Get out," he finally said. "I'm not—look…you just gotta get out. *Now*."

Darkie had no argument. She stood up and descended the shuttle steps.

"Ain't up to me, understand?" the man called after her. "I'm not—it's not that I *like*—it just ain't my call, y'see? What goes on here. Not any kinda duke or soldier or nuthin'. Just a guy." He paused, trying to form sensible words, failing. "Won't go tellin' no one's what I'm sayin'. Gotta kid sister. But just get yerself to yer bunk or what-ever. Cos if they find you and wonder how you got back here in this cold by yerself…"

His mouth clenched tight, aborting the selfish thought.

Darkie tried to remember the last time she'd seen something like that—*shame*. She smiled gratefully.

"Wandered back, got lucky." She knocked on her fore-head. "Dumb like that. Didn'tcha hear?"

She walked off without another word. But with a purpose.

Hugging her shoulders against the cold, she entered the coopyards by the main street entrance. Strolled past empty coops. Past empty shanties where handlers crowded when not handling their vicious charges. When she reached Raster's hut, she stopped. Fingers hovering nervously over the door handle.

She gently worked the door open, just enough to peep inside. As suspected, the keeper was belly down on his cot;

scraggly gray hair blanketing his grizzled face. Twitching and whimpering in a deep, sloshed sleep.

Darkie released a breath she hadn't realized she'd been holding and moved less discreetly now into the stuffy warmth of the hut, stepping over articles of clothing and refuse scattered on the wood plank floor.

She proceeded to the curtained corner where Raster let her sleep like a faithful dog (sheltering her, she dared assume, from the depravities of handlers and overmen), flung the curtain aside, ditched her serving clogs and uniform, and pulled on her old furs and ragged boots before turning back to scan Raster's room. After a moment she spotted it hanging on the back of a chair in the corner by the furnace.

Raster's utility belt.

She located the correct gadget beside the empty pocket for the leash (on loan for evening festivities), pulled it from the belt, scooped up an armful of fur garments scattered on the floor, spared Raster one last glance.

And left.

The sobbing and chattering and coughing inside the holding cell abruptly ceased when the locking mechanism clicked. The gate creaked open. Six pairs of eyes gleamed back from the dark, wild with fear...but also something else. Something Darkie thought had been smothered in the mines, in the rink, in the malevolent irony of that camp's nickname.

She saw the artless, deathless hope of children.

And with almost maternal authority, flung wide that cold steel cage.

ABOUT THE AUTHOR

TYLER BUMPUS is native to Florida, where *The Eternal Season* takes place—first volume in his post-historical saga, *The Swallowed World*. He is the sixth born of twelve children, a place in line of succession reserved (by natural order) for windbags and clowns. In spite of this, he tries to respect the time and intelligence of readers (being one himself). He is fast at work on further volumes of *The Swallowed World*.

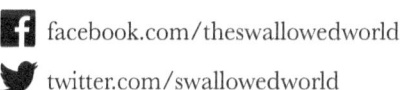

facebook.com/theswallowedworld

twitter.com/swallowedworld